WAY OF THE ODYSSEY STARTER COLLECTION

CONNOR WHITELEY

No part of this book may be reproduced in any form or by any electronic or mechanical means. Including information storage, and retrieval systems, without written permission from the author except for the use of brief quotations in a book review.

This book is NOT legal, professional, medical, financial or any type of official advice.

Any questions about the book, rights licensing, or to contact the author, please email connorwhiteley@connorwhiteley.net

Copyright © 2024 CONNOR WHITELEY

All rights reserved.

DEDICATION
Thank you to all my readers without you I couldn't do what I love.

INTRODUCTION

Sometimes there are series that stick in a writer's mind for years and years and they bug a writer until they're written. This was definitely one of those series.

So far in this *Connor Whiteley Starter Kit* series, we've looked at science fiction and fantasy and mystery. Now I want to start truly combining different genres, so we'll be exploring my favourite combination ever.

Stories that contain science fiction and fantasy elements.

If you've picked up the other volumes in the series then you know that I love fantasy because it's escapism, I love magic and I really like that sense of awe that the fantasy genre gives me. As well as I love science fiction because it allows me to explore things in the far future and that is a hell of a lot of fun.

So why not combine the two?

I've done science fiction fantasy stories a few times in my writing career and I've always loved it. I like how magic works in the far future and how that plays out, because it raises a lot of interesting questions. For example, do humans openly use magic in their advanced technology? Is magic seen as a benefit or crime in the far future? And how can magic be used to twist standard science fiction tropes?

I don't know, but that's why I write these series because they're fun and they allow my muse to explore and enjoy the offerings of both genres.

As a result, this volume focuses on a stellar, action-packed deeply unsettling science fiction fantasy series that I flat out love. It is my *Way Of The Odyssey Series*, which I cannot get enough of because they are always fun, they are always weird and they are pure escapism for me.

Also, as you know by volume 5 in this series, you'll get to enjoy twenty gripping, enthralling sci-fi fantasy short stories exploring all the weird, wonderful and dark situations that humans and alien-sympathisers find themselves in in the far future.

The story behind this series is a rather odd one to be honest, because when an idea for a series comes into my head, I just write it. Yet the idea for this series originally came to me in 2019 and I didn't start writing it until 2023, that is a long, long time for me.

And I only started writing the series because I needed more science fiction stories for a Kickstarter project that got delayed by a year, and I was including a collection with Science Fiction Fantasy Stories in. Hence, why I needed this series more than ever.

Additionally, the Way of the Odyssey series asks a few rather simple questions that I really like and I definitely think it helps to make the series fascinating.

What if humanity was ruled by a tyrannic leader that effectively brainwashed humanity into believing a magical alien race was trying to wipe out humanity, when in reality the alien race was trying to stop the resurrection of a Death God that wanted to wipe out all life in the universe?

The magical aliens effectively wanted to save humanity.

What would happen?

That was the basic idea the series sprung from and I've done over twenty short stories and two novellas in the series now with plenty more to come in the future.

To say I'm excited about that is a massive understatement.

And if you like this series then you can find all the novellas and other short stories of the series on all major eBook retailers, you can order the paperback and hardback from online retailers and your local bookstore and library if you request it. As well as you can find an audiobook version narrated by artificial intelligence for the books at selected audiobook retailers.

Or just head on over to https://www.connorwhiteleyfiction.com/way-of-the-odyssey-science-fiction-fantasy-series

So now we know more about this enthralling series, let's turn over the page and start reading some stellar stories.

CONNOR WHITELEY

AUTHOR OF AGENTS OF THE EMPEROR SERIES

CONNOR WHITELEY

TREATY OF DEFEAT

A SCIENCE FICTION FAR FUTURE SHORT STORY

TREATY OF DEFEAT

Lawyer Elaine Cars's life would be changed forever today.

Elaine sat inside her little sterile white plastic cubicle on the very top floor of her major law firm on Earth. She loved how the cubicle was always so bright, wonderful and clean unlike so many other places on Earth.

A large black holographic computer and grey hovering desk was in front of her, and Elaine really liked how the black office chair she was sitting at supported her so much better than her old one on the lower levels. She had only gotten the job promotion yesterday so this was her first full day and she seriously loved the new job so far.

It was just brilliant.

She was surprised how her new office chair seemed to cradle her body like the amazing hugs her mother used to give her before the foul cancer took her away.

And the chair supported her back, arms and neck perfectly so that Elaine was really hoping to get rid of the constant aching of her muscles from the poorly designed chairs of the awful lower levels.

Elaine was a little unsure about the sterile whiteness of the cubicle because it was a little unnerving. There was no art, paintings or pictures at all on the walls and her new boss had said that she should only be focusing on her legal work and not silly artwork.

But Elaine had always loved art ever since she was a little kid. To her, art was a way of preserving the human culture, learning about others and seeing the world in a new light.

Elaine shook away the thought and simply focused on her black holographic computer that she was seriously impressed by.

Her old one on the lower levels was so old, full and glitchy that her boss had threatened to sack her three times in the past week because apparently her productivity wasn't high enough. It was only not high enough because of the damn glitchy computer.

Thankfully that shouldn't be a problem up here on this floor, and Elaine loved how as her fingers gently touched the black holographic keyboard, the holograms no longer zapped her like her old ones did.

Every single damn night Elaine used to have to put her fingertips in a tub of ice to stop the pain, the zapping was that painful, but hopefully that wouldn't be a problem now.

Elaine clicked on her computer and was surprised that her caseload was so small today.

When she was working on the lower floors, she used to work forty cases a day and mostly she failed a ton of clients like every single other lawyer on Earth but she liked to believe she tried her hardest on all her cases. It was only yesterday she had helped keep a family together so they weren't ripped apart, she had also helped a family get their innocent daughter off a murder charge and she had convicted a kidnapper.

She helped so many amazing people and that was why she loved her job so much but she wanted to help even more people.

"Welcome Elaine to the Top Criminal Division of Baring & Law," her computer said.

Elaine felt so excited to finally be able to access the top-secret and highly sensitive and dangerous cases that these legendary lawyers dealt with.

But when she went to click on her inbox she watched all her other cases disappear and she was only left with a single case.

She clicked on it.

It was really odd that it took a while for the case file to open and Elaine detected a subtle change in the air. The environmental systems on Earth were meant to be the best in the Imperium but now all she could smell was sugar, caramel and candyfloss. It was a wonderful smell if not a little strange, yet she did love the taste of salted caramel that formed on her tongue.

"Access granted," the computer said.

Elaine had no idea why she needed access to look at her own workload but she didn't care and she simply looked at the file.

She instantly frowned as she read the file. She was going to have to deal with a female Keres, a foul alien abomination that had committed an awful crime against humanity and the Imperium.

Elaine hated the Keres with a passion, they were always so rude, foul and just beasts when compared to humanity. And they were just freaks as well with their magic and Elaine shivered in fear.

It was a very well-known rule in the Imperium that humans should never ever mix with such awful creatures that were sadly allowed to roam around in the Imperium because of the Treaty of Defeat.

The only piece of comfort that Elaine and all of humanity got from the Treaty was that the Keres were certainly second-class citizens and they were to be discriminated against at every single chance that presented itself.

Elaine actually wasn't so sure that was fair or just or right but she was a lawyer now and it was her task to make sure this Keres scum plead guilty to charges of theft.

It was so damn annoying that this scum felt like she had the right to steal from superior humans. That was disgraceful and Elaine was so looking forward to punishing this alien beast.

But she couldn't help but feel like there was more to this story and as much as she wanted to believe everything the Imperium said about the Keres.

She had actually never met one before and she couldn't help but believe there was a tiny chance they weren't everything the posters said they were.

But right now all Elaine was interested in was protecting humanity from the aliens.

***

Because the Keres were such foul, dangerous and awful creatures, Elaine was really glad they were kept in high-security areas of the law firm so she had to go through more security checkpoints than she cared to think about.

Elaine went down a very long black metal corridor with prison bars lining the corridor and the disgusting Keres prisoners were standing there looking so scared at her, with bright blue prison collars around their awful necks.

Elaine absolutely hated the Keres' appearance. They were humanoid in shape but their chests and waists were a lot thinner and their facial features were more angled and she might have even classed the very fit men handsome if they weren't alien scum.

All the Keres wore black prisoner uniforms that fit their very slim and spinney bodies very well.

Just like everyone else in the Imperium Elaine had lived through the War between humans and Keres, and just like the news reports said Elaine had to agree that the Keres were monsters.

The aliens burnt entire planets in the name of their Empire, they murdered every human they came over and they used their magic for such dark purposes that Elaine often turned off the news at night. All whilst humanity was being angelic, calm and wonderful.

They never killed a Keres that didn't deserve it.

Elaine kept walking down the long corridor until she reached the end of it where a steel door was that opened for her only. She went inside.

The interrogation room was perfect for the female Keres scum that sat on a cold metal chair and rested on her long thin arms on the metal table. Thankfully she was chained and Elaine was not going to order the guards to release her.

The Keres were way too dangerous for that. And Elaine just had to focus on how badly she wanted to protect her friends, family and species from these foul aliens.

As Elaine sat down on the icy cold chair and tucked it in, she had to admit she was surprised that the Keres female looked so scared, human and innocent.

Yet that was something else that the glorious Rex pointed out about the awful Keres, they were masters of fear and manipulation. Elaine couldn't dare allow herself to be manipulated by the alien.

She had to remain strong to protect her species. And all she needed to do was get a confession and then go.

"You are accused of theft," Elaine said.

The Keres looked at her. "Please. I didn't steal anything. The human gave it to me,"

Elaine laughed. "That's what they all say and we all know you Keres are thieves,"

The female Keres shook her head as Elaine got out her holo-slate and looked at the case notes she had made in the lift.

"You were found with two hundred Guards worth of technological gadgets that you stole from a merchant," Elaine said.

"No," the Keres said. "I bought that equipment fair and square. I showed the Justice the receipt and he logged it into evidence,"

Elaine nodded because she wasn't lying and there was a receipt.

"I know but the Treaty of Defeat made it clear. The law states that if a Keres buys something then it doesn't belong to Keres. And if the human wants it back then the Keres must give it back without refund,"

The Keres's foul lips thinned. "I know that but…"

Elaine just couldn't understand how this alien could understand the law and so willingly break it. That was why no one liked the Keres.

It wasn't exactly a confession and Elaine sadly knew it wouldn't make her bosses happy with her.

"It just isn't fair," she said.

Elaine stopped for a moment. She had been given this case to get a guilty verdict and she needed this piece of scum to confess, but she highly doubted she would get it if she didn't fake trust and liking this piece of criminal trash.

Elaine forced herself to smile and looked at the alien. All she needed to do was get the alien to trust her and confess to her crime completely.

"Why did you buy it then?" Elaine asked, trying to sound how she did with humans.

The Keres looked at her like Elaine was a good friend. Elaine really couldn't believe how this species had gotten so powerful if they broke laws and trusted so easily.

"It's my husband's birthday today so I was going to get him a special treat. He fought for the humans in the War and he had always loved those old holo-movies so I was hoping to record one for myself and show him. I have a degree in Keres Film Studies,"

Elaine forced herself not to shiver. The Glorious Rex had shown the Imperium what the Keres called "movies" and it was horrific. There was so much blood, murder and other things that she didn't even want to think about.

And apparently what humans called horror films were comedies to the Keres. That was how messed up the aliens were.

Elaine forced herself to nod and smile. "That's really nice of you. I wished my husband did that for me,"

She didn't have a husband but she had learnt over the years if you wanted to make someone trust you, tell them you were in a relationship. It worked every time.

"Thank you. So I saved for months and months and I travelled here on a cargo shuttle to get the equipment,"

Elaine frowned. "You came on a method of transport that wasn't a dedicated Keres flight?"

The female Keres frowned slightly. "Um, it wasn't that serious. I only wanted to cross into Imperial Space for a day and the Keres flights are two hundred times the price of a cargo shuttle,"

Elaine shook her head. "I'm sorry but the Treaty is clear. Keres can only come into Imperial Space if they board a dedicated Keres flight. It is illegal for you to come on any other transport method,"

The Keres frowned. "And yet you humans can use any method to come into our Empire. You can teleport, use cargo shuttles, tourist shuttles and military transports. How is that fair?"

Elaine shrugged because this wasn't her problem. She only wanted to protect her friends, family and species from the Keres.

The law helped her do that.

The Keres tried to reach across the table but she couldn't and Elaine was so glad about that.

"Please. This isn't right. I pay for those goods, I might not have returned them when asked but that was because this isn't right. The Keres are victimised at every single turn,"

As much as Elaine wanted to leave because she had her confession, she actually wanted to listen for just a moment longer. Because emotionally she couldn't understand where the hell this whacko alien was coming from, but at an intelligence and rational level, the alien made a good point.

"Your species signed the Treaty of Defeat. They could have chosen not to. If you're mad at the laws you are subject to then be mad at your Creator or whatever weird name you have for him,"

The Keres shook her head. "You lie and you don't know your own history. The Keres were forced to sign those documents or your humanity was going to nuke our entire Empire and ten planets of your own,"

Elaine laughed. This alien needed to be locked away desperately. She was a psycho.

"Our Creator could live with the sacrifice and defeat of our species but we wouldn't allow your Rex to annihilate hundreds of billions of his own people and he knew that,"

Elaine just laughed because this alien was just making up so many excuses for her criminal actions, but she couldn't help but feel like she wasn't lying.

Her father had served in the War and even though he had come back a changed man because of the things he had seen, he had been drunk one night and he had mentioned about killing humans.

Elaine had always dismissed the memory but what if her father wasn't wrong?

She just looked at the foul alien scum and shook her head. This wasn't right and this was just another manipulation that the Keres was using on her.

She had her confession and thankfully this alien was going to be locked away for a very, very long time.

Elaine got up to leave but the Keres spoke to her. "I feel sorry for humanity because your Rex pumps out so much hate, propaganda and lies that even you cannot tell the difference between right and wrong. Oh, wow humanity has lost its way,"

Elaine just left the scum in the room because she didn't have time for any more lies.

But deep, deep down Elaine had to admit that the Keres might not be wrong after all.

***

After a great, wonderful and sensational day of working another ten more cases involving the disgusting Keres, Elaine sat back on her delightful chair and sterile white cubicle that stopped her from seeing the other workers that had their own white cubicles and Elaine had to admit today had been weird.

Her bosses had said how great, ruthless and cunning she was because she had managed to get a confession from each of the Keres criminals, but the words of the first Keres had only grown in her mind with each case.

She had interrogated and charged all ten of the other Keres today and if she really had to admit it, they were all for silly petty crimes that humans couldn't actually get charged for.

Like her last case was charging a Keres for "assaulting" a human when all that had actually happened was the Keres had been tripped over by an elderly woman and the male Keres had fallen on top of a female teenager.

The Keres had been arrested and Elaine had charged him for a hundred years to be served on a mining world by making him do forced labour.

And as the wonderful smells of mint, lavender and caramel formed in the air, Elaine couldn't help but wonder if this was right in the slightest. And each of the Keres had told her differing stories to how the Keres Empire had come to sign onto the Treaty of Defeat and none of them matched the Rex's version.

Was it possible that Elaine was lied to?

Elaine had no idea and if she was thinking about this from a legal and historical viewpoint (because she had studied history briefly before the Rex outlawed history) she had to admit it was very, very possible.

But that was a problem for another day, Elaine was one woman in one law firm on one planet of the Imperium. She couldn't do anything about it and if she didn't convict Keres people then she couldn't get paid.

Yet she couldn't deny that it wasn't fair so maybe, just maybe one day she could help change all of that but it was a very, very long way away and Elaine had a large amount of criminals to deal with first.

So Elaine had to return to the job and caseload she loved with a new sense of injustice that she knew would morph into action at some point and the Keres would be saved.

AUTHOR OF AGENTS OF THE EMPEROR SERIES

CONNOR WHITELEY

ENEMY OF HISTORY

A SCIENCE FICTION FAR FUTURE SHORT STORY

ENEMY OF HISTORY

Librarian Aria Pinncock had always loved her library with its immense wooden shelves and dark varnish that stretched on for hundreds of miles and the tourists flocked to see the library just for the shelves alone. You couldn't see wooden shelves anywhere else in the Imperium, and Aria really did love the soft blue carpet. It was just such a strange texture that also wasn't found anywhere else in the Imperium.

She stood on the very bottom of the great wooden staircase that went elegantly up towards the second, third and fourth floors of the immense library that she had come to love so much. The staircase was a real beaut with its solid oak railing that were handcrafted on Earth itself with all sorts of designs that the Rex personally approved for the library.

Aria wasn't really sure that she liked it when the tourists said that the staircase was holy or something because the Rex had apparently touched it himself. But considering just how much propaganda there was in the Imperium, it was impossible to tell.

Aria still loved her job.

The staircase even had a couple of marks, scratches and worn patches where so many great scholars had been working away and going up and down to investigate their latest project.

Aria really had enjoyed her career in academia and she had always liked this library even more. Especially with its rows upon rows of real blue leather-bound hardbacks, as the Head Librarian

Aria was always searching for more but most of the books she bought were confiscated by the Rex.

Damn him.

It was always such a rarity to see real print books these days with their soft leather covers, musty smell and cold to the touch that Aria never wanted to leave her library. It was a place of knowledge and she had seen the first-hand impacts of the Rex's great campaign to suppress knowledge.

People talking, muttering and even shouting caught Aria's attention as a large group of white robbed scholars were walking towards the staircase. Aria didn't allow them to worry her for now.

Aria had gone on holiday plenty of times to the other systems without a librarian like herself that prized knowledge beyond all else. So many millions of people died because their medical care was shambolic, all because the Rex had suppressed important medical textbooks because of the so-called evil knowledge inside certain passages.

Apparently the Rex was going to rewrite all the books he confiscated but Aria had never seen such books.

It was why she had been kicked out of academia and she had lost her history job, her fellow professors and best friends were imprisoned for not agreeing to rewrite history books for Rex and she actually had no idea what happened to them. Aria was only saved because a few decades ago her family were rich, powerful and the Rex liked them a great deal.

Aria hadn't spoken to them for decades, she just wanted to keep them safe. When she started learning about history she never ever imagined it would become a crime.

"Excuse me," a man said.

Aria looked at the man and forced herself not to frown at the four white robed men that looked awful in their sterile white cloth robes that meant they were from the Rex's personal university on Earth. These men were probably the most indoctrinated people in the Imperium into the cult of the Rex's lies, deceit and corruption.

She couldn't allow these people to do anything against her, her library or any of the thousands of people on all the floors. She had to protect them.

The sweet aromas of pine, cherry and apples filled Aria's senses leaving the wonderful taste of warm apple pie on her tongue just like how her mother had baked when she was a child. Her mother would have hated what the Rex had done to history.

"Yes, what can I do for you fine gentleman?" Aria asked.

Aria noticed that she couldn't see any of the men's faces. It was like they were shrouded in a form of shadow that wasn't dark nor light.

"We are seeking a book called the Enlighted Bible," one of the men said.

Aria slowly nodded making it seem like she was searching her memories. Of course she knew exactly what book they were referring to, it was her favourite purchase this year, a book confirming the existence of a breakaway democratic republic of humans away from the Rex's control.

That was an amazing find so she couldn't allow these stupid men to find the book and destroy it.

"That book is a danger to the safety of the Imperium," another man said. "That book contains knowledge that has the potential to shake the Imperium to its core and cause a civil war,"

Aria seriously doubted that because she had read the first few pages (more than enough to get her killed) and the book was just describing a life of freedom, learning and pleasure in the solar systems controlled by the Enlightened Republic.

"I do not know of this book," Aria said, knowing she was done for.

Aria looked around in some vain hope of trying to find an escape path or something but there wasn't one. She knew every single inch of this library and there was no escape. She already had a feeling there were more white robed men on other floors just waiting for her to escape.

And those men would kill her.

"I just wanted to learn about the past, learning is not a crime," Aria said.

The men laughed and the tallest of the men stepped forward and arrested Aria, handcuffing her with holographic cuffs.

"Aria Pinncock you are an Enemy of The True History of Humanity and you are a terrorist trying to spread lies and corruption about the Great Rex," he said.

Aria just laughed as the men led her away and she quickly realised that she had to escape no matter what because these men would interrogate her to find the book.

But once they had the book they would kill her.

**

The awful aromas of burnt petrol, ozone and death filled Aria's senses as she leant against the icy cold black metal wall of the interrogation chamber. She was half expecting something grander considering these people were most probably the top-secret organisation known as the *Erasers*.

But the interrogation chamber was nothing more than a black metal box without a table or chair or very good environmental systems it turned out. It was just all rather uncreative but she supposed that was the point.

She, like everyone else in the Imperium, knew that if someone was picked up by the Erasers then they really were as good as dead and the Erasers on the interrogation ship were in constant communication with the ground force. So sooner or later the book would be found by the ground force and whoever came to interrogate her would kill her.

And it was even worse that the interrogations always happened on a big bulky circular ship that always struck fear in the hearts of humans whenever they saw it. Aria really hated it how she was now on one of those damn ships.

Aria had no idea whatsoever if she had done enough to hide the book. All she actually wanted was to finish reading it, learning about it and developing her knowledge about what the galaxy was really like instead of what the Rex wanted her to believe.

"Do not attack," a female computerised voice said.

Aria stood up perfectly straight as the deafening roar of a faulty teleportation hummed around the chamber.

A moment later a very tall white robed woman appeared, she looked the same as the men but her boots were black and she actually had her hood up.

And Aria couldn't help but feel like she was hearing a strange sound in the background but she couldn't quite identify what it was.

"You are currently listening to psycho-conditioning files making you more likely to tell me the location of the book," the woman said coldly. "You are a terrorist and you will die but how quickly and painfully is down to you,"

Aria just couldn't understand how the hell the Imperium had actually gotten like this, it was just impossible to imagine how an Imperium that loved, treasured and worshipped learning and history had gone so backwards so quickly.

"I will not allow you to destroy knowledge," Aria said.

The woman laughed. "Knowledge is nothing more than a weapon. Whoever controls knowledge controls people. The Rex controls knowledge so he controls every human in the Imperium and he basically controls the Keres too,"

Aria bit her lip at the sheer mention of alien Keres. A poor innocent alien race with beautiful magic that the Rex had decided were a threat so he bullied them into a war and submission and crippled a peaceful race.

Aria hated it when she had learnt the truth about the Keres, but sadly that history book had been burnt by a "friend" of hers. She was so glad she pushed him through an airlock, by accident of course.

"I will ask you three times a simple question and if you do not tell me after the third question I will kill you using crippling pain. Where is the book?"

Aria looked around. She had barely any time to free herself and she really had no intention of dying today.

Her former husband that died a few years ago fighting the Keres in the futile war would have wanted her to go out and find love again. And her mother would want her to protect history.

"Okay then you are refusing to answer me," the woman said.

Aria focused on the seams of the interrogation chamber but the damn workmanship was so fine that the entire chamber seemed to be moulded from a single sheet of steel.

There were no weak points.

Aria stood up and started tapping the walls.

"You will not find anything. Where is the book?"

Aria frowned. She really was running out of time to escape and then she realised that she was a history professor first and foremost regardless of whatever the Rex said.

Two hundred years ago when the Erasers were first founded, Aria read an article and interview written by an escapee before she was brutally burnt alive but she wrote that no one watched the interrogations and the only people who could escape were the interrogators.

That was what Aria needed to focus on. And because the woman had teleported in, she had to have a teleporter on her.

Aria just looked at the woman and smiled. The woman seemed to shudder.

Aria went over to the woman and placed her hands around her neck. The woman didn't seem to react but Aria pulled her hood down. Revealing the woman had a cybernetic eye so someone was watching her.

"You read the interview too then," the woman said. "I was like you once but no one escapes this place,"

Aria spat at the woman as she realised the so-called escapee was just a trap to lure idiots like her to their deaths. But her plan was still going to work.

Aria punched the woman, smashing her eye so no one else was watching them and she knew she only had moments left before someone checked on her.

Aria quickly changed clothes with the woman and made sure that the hood was up on her and the woman interrogator was dressed in her clothes.

A moment later three large black armoured humans appeared and Aria just looked at them with such a fierce aura of authority that the men actually bowed at her.

Aria really loved the technology that shrouded her face from the men's glare.

"She is dead. Let us leave," Aria said.

The men nodded and the deafening roar of a faulty teleportation filled the air and Aria just smiled as she teleported away and now she just needed to escape this ship before her deception was found out.

***

A few hours later, Aria crawled up into a small little ball inside the large(ish) bright white pod of a space shuttle that she had stolen from the Eraser Ship. She had tried to disable the tracker, the autopilot and all the rest of the annoying things that the Imperium installed on their shuttles and ships to make sure people like her didn't steal them, but she wasn't sure.

She had been flying for about an hour and the circular Eraser Ship didn't seem to be tracking her or anything so it seemed to be okay for now. Aria just wanted to get away from the Imperium, the Rex's forces and actually just wanted freedom.

The pod shuttle was thankfully simple and it wasn't too hard to figure out it worked with only a few bright white holograms forming her commands for her.

She had already worked out how to make the shuttle speed up, slow down and turn a little so hopefully that was everything she really needed to know for the moment. The pod also had some great environmental systems with the sweet senses of apple pie, pecans and oranges filling the air and after being interrogated it was such a relaxing smell.

As Aria watched the pitch darkness of space slowly go past her with bright white stars in the distance and a handful of planets from her home system going past, Aria just smiled because she might have been a criminal now and an enemy of the Rex's true history, but she was free.

Freedom was a myth in the Imperium and now Aria could finally go out and seek the amazing Enlightened Republic. She would live there, get to taste their way of life and most importantly she would get to learn what history was actually like.

Because the Rex could always try to take the girl out of history, but it was impossible to take the history out of the girl. And that was why she loved being an enemy of history.

AUTHOR OF AGENTS OF THE EMPEROR SERIES

CONNOR WHITELEY

WATCHING THE WRECK

A SCIENCE FICTION FAR FUTURE SHORT STORY

WATCHING THE WRECK

When I, Mila Scott, was younger I actually loved going into the cold, darkness of space with my brothers and sisters flying about in our junker of a space shuttle. An awful little pod-like object that I was always scared of it falling apart, that was exactly how old it was. Me and my sisters and brothers saw some wonderful things in the Imperium, massive stars, circular battleships and little bright white pods that tried to kill us once or twice.

Those really were the days of our youth that I absolutely loved. Then as we all grew older, a little fatter and not a lot wiser, we all went our separate and rather different ways.

My three brothers they joined the Imperial Army and all died during the stupid war with the peaceful aliens known as the Keres, all because our stupid leader the Rex was scared of their magic. They all died.

My sisters went to study medicine on Earth, a so-called great honour but because both of them were certainly daughters of our mother, they questioned way too much and I think the Erasers killed them so others wouldn't question the Rex's version of events.

That's the silly galaxy we live in.

And as for little old me, well I was stupid enough to study history and become a history graduate, I even have a PhD in Early Imperium Studies and the Rex hates that subject.

That's why I'm sitting pretty at my bright white metal desk inside my even whiter cubicle with its awfully smooth walls that I hate, and

I'm having to stare at a little holographic computer screen.

Thankfully, there's a small red dot flashing at the very, very edge of my computer screen but until it gets closer towards the centre of my screen, I really don't want to do anything about it.

Personally I just want to add some holo-art of something to the perfectly smooth walls but I cannot. Apparently that would endanger my life, it's rubbish of course but I always like to see their excuses for controlling every single aspect of my life.

The cubicle itself isn't so bad I suppose, there's a brand-new small single bed that is rather comfortable, it just sits behind me during the day and it doubles as a sofa and dining table. The people in charge here don't exactly give you much.

Granted, I hate its soft blue sheets because I could have sworn the bosses here coat the material in a waxy substance that annoys me when I go to sleep. I also flat out the little food shoot, that really is nothing more than a metal pipe that drops food into my cubicle.

I mean I am no dog, cat or animal so why can't I just get given food like every other normal person in the Imperium. Normally food is just shipped to entire planets from Farming Worlds but clearly that might not happen here.

And the smell is just the worse at feeding time, because the pipe connects directly outside the cubicle gets filled with the disgusting senses of burnt ozone, petrol and raw meat. It flat out isn't a nice place, I hate it.

"Three minutes until Exercise Time," a loud computerised voice said.

Oh yes, if you can believe it. The bosses here actually give us very set exercise time, it's basically the only ten minutes we're allowed to leave these cubicles each day. And that's why I'm so excited about when I can finally leave this form of prison.

Officially, when the Rex decided to outlaw history (because it was the only thing that could challenge his lies), he arrested, killed and captured all the history professionals in the Imperium. I was one of the "Lucky" few that got to enlist in the army and now I am stuck on this awful military moon just watching the border between the Imperium and the dying Keres Empire.

In other words, I get to stare at pitch darkness all day.

And my mother said studying history was a brilliant idea.

The wonderful sounds of my friends (my other inmates) laughing, talking and discussing what they're found on their computer screens is loud enough to get through the thick white walls, and I'm so looking forward to seeing them.

Even ten minutes with them is a wonderful distraction to the mind numbing pain of this prison.

I get up and past my bed where the wall should dissolve and I should be able to go outside.

"Not for you. You have an object on your screen. You must sort it out first before going for your exercise time, no extra time will be given," the computerised voice said.

I wanted to smash my fists into a wall or something. How dare this stupid voice and my bosses deduct my exercise time from me just because of some dumb red spot.

I went back over to my computer screen and tapped my fingers on the spot.

I read the output as the tapping always gave me a light reading and scan of whatever the object was. It was certainly Imperium in nature, I would recognise the black circular design anywhere.

But the materials were all wrong, and my knowledge of history and my wonderful relationship with a boy studying Military History (he was one that got a bullet in the head by the Rex), I knew these materials haven't been used in two thousand years to build Imperium ships.

I zoom in even more because I just couldn't understand this, this ship is coming in the direction of the Keres Empire and yet this is an Imperium vessel.

The Keres Empire have always, always been peaceful, magical and great aliens that truly respect humanity, well unlike humanity determined to slaughter them, and even the most extreme elements of Keres society (that only came about because of the war) would never keep an Imperium vessel and then return it later on.

That was a very human thing to do.

"Computer," I said, "I need access to the others,"

"Access denied. You are a Level 5 Operative, you do not need lessers to help you," the voice said.

Damn it. I seriously hated my bosses, and part of the problem was that I actually was that good unfortunately so the bosses trusted me. I had sadly stopped a number of smuggling ships trying to bring Keres refugees into Imperial space so they could get food, medical supplies and clean water for their people.

All things that the Imperium had stolen from them after the war.

I zoomed in and really focused on the circular ship and I started to scan it deeply. I had to know what was going on here.

The ship had no power, no engines, no weapon systems. All of it had been taken out and that actually was a rather Keres thing to do because it helped them to maintain the peace, but there were also no bodies.

Typically, and the Rex would never admit this, the Keres always used their magic to knock out the human attackers so they could enter a peaceful sleep and then the Keres would return the attackers to the Imperium.

That was partly why they lost the war. Their commitment to peace was amazing if not their downfall.

Then a single reading popped up and I just smiled. It turned out there was a single corpse on the ship and it proved everything I ever wanted to do about the ship.

There was an Imperial corpse on the ship, meaning a murder had taken place and if there was one thing my bosses hated it was a dead body.

Now I just needed to play it to my advantage.

I just hoped that the computer and my bosses had forgotten how me and my friends were all excellent coders and we could easily manipulate a hologram system to scan for whatever we want. It was amazing the skills you could pick up.

I could easily do this work on my own but I just wanted to see my friends and most importantly I wanted to see if there was a chance of escape.

I didn't want to be stuck on this damn moon anymore.

"Computer, I need access to the others now. There's a dead human on that ship and if killers are onboard then we have to know before it reaches Imperial Space," I said, hoping beyond hope it would work.

There was a long pause.

"Granted. Doors will open now and everyone will meet in the Command Centre," the voice said.

I weakly smiled, not only because I was going to get a chance to see my friends but also because the Command Centre was where our captors or "bosses" were. And I had always known some of my friends wanted their freedom.

Maybe this was the time to fight for our freedom too.

***

Now granted, I have never been to the command centre before but I would have imagined it was a little more high-tech than this junk.

I was standing in nothing more than a large dirty white cubicle about four times bigger than my own cubicle, so it was still rather small. There were barely any holograms, and the only white holograms there were were about the weather, not something I'm very interested in knowing about on a moon.

There was a small porthole that was just showed how the bright orange rock of the moon stretched on endlessly with craters, unexploded bombs and our cubicles punctuating the orange rock.

It was not pretty.

Thankfully, there was a huge holographic table in the middle of the command centre showing a large flickering depiction of the black circular wreck I had found earlier.

And all my friends were here, which was amazing.

There were only five other people here out of ten, so I was a little worried about where they were but I didn't mind.

My best friend in the entire galaxy, Paula was standing next to me in her normal pink jeans, hoody and boots. She was more than ready to work.

"This is a wreck from two centuries before the Keres War," a man called Andy said, sporting a very dirty jacket that looked like it was about to fall apart at any moment.

"But how did it end up behind Keres lines?" Paula said.

"Well I don't know what we can say without getting killed," James said, a very short man.

I smiled because that was the truth of it. We could all easily solve this mystery if we were allowed to discuss history but of course that would only get us all killed.

And I really didn't like the gentle humming of the command centre, almost like our bosses were preparing to gas us all at a moment's notice.

"Wait, so we all know if we don't solve this mystery with the wreck, we don't get fed tonight but could this be an opportunity?" I said.

Well, if our bosses were going to gas us anyway, I at least wanted to know if the others wanted freedom.

"From what I remember, the Imperium has always used the other basic communication network," Andy said.

I nodded as I swiped the holographic table a few times and tried to establish a connection with the wreck. Then I remembered how it didn't have any power.

The holographic table flashed and a small warning hologram came up. It was saying the scan had just been scanned by a magical sign.

"There's Keres on that ship," Paula said, failing to show her excitement.

I didn't want to comment as I heard the command centre humming even louder and the others were starting to show their own concern at the sound.

If I wanted to make sure me and my friends survived this then I had to be very careful here. The problem was that this command centre was set to kill us so we could never escape and pass on our historical knowledge to anyone else. Including the Keres.

Another problem was that the Keres were sending a wreckage towards us and I don't know why.

And to make things even worse, my friends were building their assumption on the Keres were here to save us. What if they weren't?

But as the humming of the command centre reached a deafening level, I just knew I couldn't wait around for answers. We needed to escape now, ideally find our bosses and kill them.

"Cannons activating," a computerised voice said.

"Damn it," I said.

Our bosses were preparing to destroy the wreckage so the Keres died and we couldn't escape. Damn them. Damn the Rex. Damn the Imperium.

As one me and my friends all started typing on the holographic table and tried to access the moon's central mainframe so we could access all computer systems on the moon.

"I did it," Paula said.

I moved round to her set of holograms. I was the best coder amongst all of us so I took control.

Our bosses were fighting us and trying to force us out but they were thinking I was going after the cannons.

I wasn't.

Our bosses kicked out everyone else from the system but I was here logged in. I was going after the gas and environmental systems that would ultimately kill us.

I found them. Then I programmed the environmental systems to pump the toxic gas into the chamber where my bosses were.

The system complied and the loud deafening screams of my bosses echoed around the command centre as I played the audio from their chamber beneath us.

My friends laughed, hugged each other and I loved their sheer happiness but I had to save the Keres. The cannons were still being activated and then the results of a much better scan came in that Andy had started running in secret.

There were thousands of Keres refugees on the ship that had been using their magic to shield themselves from scanning. And in fact the entire wreckage wasn't Imperial in nature, it was a beautifully, bejewelled stunning Keres battleship.

I had to save those innocent people.

I found the cannons. They were about to fire.

I hit the kill code but it didn't work.

I tried changing the target.

It didn't work.

So I tried to kill the power.

All the power on the moon deactivated and everything went perfectly silent and it was only in the sheer deadly silence of the moon that I realised just how much background noise I had tuned out since I got here.

But that included the environmental systems were off too.

And it wasn't like I could reactivate the power because the cannon commands were still in the computer system waiting to be carried out the moment there was power again.

I just looked at all my amazing friends, Paula, Andy and the rest. They all looked so shocked but they were smiling.

Not because they were happy about dying on some moon that they hated, but because they were going to sacrifice themselves so innocent people could live.

I was damn proud of them.

My lungs jerked as I tried to breathe in air that wasn't there and then my lungs burnt painfully as they screamed out for air. Air that was never coming for them.

I was about to shut my eyes and allow the darkness of death to claim me when I felt a warm magical energy wrap around me and my vision was blinded by a beautiful golden light.

***

When I opened my eyes again, I couldn't exactly understand why I was laying down on something hard, light blue and oddly warm but it was nice, so much nicer than anything human I had ever felt.

I pushed myself and allowed my legs to dangle over the edge, and I was pleased that it was a sort of medical table that I had been sitting on. It looked like it was made from a yellow sort of plastic but the Keres were always masters of technology and making things. This was probably a material I had never thought of before.

The medical chamber itself was stylish and like a massive pod with beautiful baby blue walls with the artist's brush marks swirling, twirling and whirling around each other. It was so beautiful to look at and even the jewelled ceiling with diamonds, rubies and stranger, more alien gems was simply stunning.

The quiet humming, laughing and talking of my best friends gave me such relief. At least they were alive, well and seemingly very happy so at least I didn't get everyone killed, and it was only now that I was realising exactly what we had done.

We had saved so many innocent people from dying a painful death, we had finally escaped our bosses and that damn moon so now the Imperium could no longer watch their precious border with the Keres Empire in case an invasion even happened.

But it wouldn't and I was okay with that because me and my friends were free.

The sweet smells of oranges, jasmine and lemons filled the air as a section of the wall dissolved and in came a very thin and male Keres. He was humanoid in shape and features but he was much tall, almost dangerously thin and he certainly looked a lot more regal than humans ever could.

"Thank you," the male Keres said bowing elegantly.

"No, thank you for saving us. You can drop us off wherever, me and my friends don't want to burden you,"

The Keres laughed so beautifully that it was like listening to a melody. "Now it seems you are being silly because your crew have already accepted an offer of employment, and I hope you will accept it too. Live with us and join us and become one of us or yes, we will drop you off whenever you desire,"

If this person wasn't Keres then I naturally would have denied it because this was a very dangerous offer. But I am a history professor and Doctor of History, I know that the Keres are deeply caring, supportive and protective people and they will always see me and my crew as one of them.

If we live with the Keres then we will never be in danger from them, they will live freely and we can actually experience joy once more. And I want that so badly.

"I accept," I said bowing to the Keres as that was their equivalent of a handshake.

"Excellent, your friends are in the dining chamber playing, I think you call it, carks?"

Because he was being so nice to me, my friends and he had offered us freedom and joy after a lifetime of pain, I didn't care to correct him. But as I left the medical chamber, I was looking forward to playing *cards*, starting my new life and finally start watching the Imperium from the other side and I have to admit it really will be like watching a wreckage that would never enslave me again.

Because I wouldn't let it.

AUTHOR OF AGENTS OF THE EMPEROR SERIES

CONNOR WHITELEY

FARMING RESTRICTION

A SCIENCE FICTION FAR FUTURE SHORT STORY

FARMING RESTRICTIONS

Farming Director Adam Grant leant against the wonderfully warm balcony made from soft, sweet marble that was freshly shipped in from some random colony that he didn't care about. The soft refreshing, slightly warm breath brushed his cheeks and he was so looking forward to today.

His balcony was attached to an immense circular spaceship painted black that hovered just off the hard, cracked ground of Ceres 14. A beautifully lush planet most of the time but right now, that statement was in question.

For as far as Adam could see the ground was yellow, hard and cracked and it made no sense at all considering it rained twice a week on this planet, just as the glorious Rex had designed it. The latest data suggested the dryness of the planet was spreading a little too quickly for Adam's liking and sooner or later it would be impossible to grow crops on.

It was also strange and a little confusing that the large mountains and rolling hills of the planet that had been filled with olive trees, vegetables and more only yesterday were now completely empty, and the hills were mostly flat.

He supposed there could have been some kind of environmental reason for it all, but Adam had been working here for two decades now and this had never happened before. The environmental systems that destroyed the planet's natural weather systems were in perfect working order so all of this should have been impossible.

Adam really enjoyed the large, fat sun beaming down on him sending gentle warmth through his body and the sweet smells of corn, strawberries and honey filling the air from the latest harvest.

Possibly the last harvest for a long while.

Adam hated to imagine what Earth and the Rex would say when news of their crisis reached them. All Adam had wanted was a nice position of watching fruit, vegetables and livestock grow and he might have to do some paperwork from time to time but clearly he was actually going to have to do something.

He flat out hated the idea of that. And he hated the implications of the dryness of the planet even more. Everyone in the Imperium knew that the Rex only delivered food and water to planets that showed the most devotion to him and their dedication to rewrite history in his image.

It was only a month ago when he had been ordered to deliver two warships filled the most nutritious vegetables to reward a mining colony for killing all their history professors and over two thousand rebels who hated the Rex's rule.

Adam didn't agree with rewarding murder and bloodshed in the slightest but the Rex was the ruler of the Imperium and until anyone had the balls to rise up against him. Nothing would ever change in the Imperium.

And things would only continue to get worse and worse. Adam hated it how he had already been ordered to *decrease* food production by 20% over the past year to "give the populous of the Imperium more incentive to worship the Rex".

Adam's hands formed fists at the very notion of him not being able to do his job and actually have to make innocent people starve because of the Rex's twisted ideology. It was bad enough that the Imperium only allowed food to be grown on Farming Worlds that were highly, highly regulated but it was just stupid to have every single thing Adam did watched and approved by Earth.

Earth was just stupid.

"Chief," a woman said behind him.

Adam forced himself not to jump as the woman's voice sliced through the relaxing silence of the warm morning, he had wanted to enjoy the peace for a few more moments but that was never going to happen with a crisis unfolding around him.

Especially when he turned to face the woman and he was surprised she was wearing the black battle armour of the Imperial Army. Her medals and stripes and crowns on her armour told Adam everything he needed to know.

He was in the presence of one of the Imperium's high-ranking military officers. She was a Lord Commander, probably the Lord Commander of this entire sector of space and that never ended well.

As she came over to Adam and leant next to him, he had to admit with her long beautiful eyelashes, perfect smile and smooth skin she was certainly beautiful. Even her jasmine-scented perfume was a luxury Adam could never afford so why was a very rich and well-to-do commander visiting his little slice of hell?

"I was sent by Earth directly to investigate the matter of your planet," the woman said. "I am Lord Commander Isabella Coze,"

Adam forced himself not to frown as she said her name. Everyone, even the people living under rocks, knew of Commander Coze and how she enjoyed watching entire planets, races and populations get burnt alive for the smallest of infractions against the Imperium.

If she was here then his fate was already sealed. Not including the fate of all his workers, crops and the billions of people that relied on his food production.

"The Rex proposes that you have broken many Farming Restrictions and this is His Will and Plan to make you suffer," Coze said.

Adam shook his head. He knew that the Rex believed himself to be some kind of deranged god but he wasn't. And it was flat out impossible that Rex and his so-called divine power could reach through hundreds of thousands of solar systems to Ceres just to make the planet dry.

And if Coze believed it then she was a dick.

"I do not believe him," Coze said. "I believe there is a real cause to this planet's problems and whilst I am under rules to command you to build churches to the Rex. I am more concerned about my own military's food supply,"

Adam made sure his face didn't react because even Coze just admitting the Rex was wrong was more than enough to earn her a very slow, painful and agonising death.

"Where did the problems start?" Coze asked.

Adam shook his head. "They didn't. Everything just happened in front of my worker's eyes working the night shift last night. All three affected areas of the planet were impacted at once,"

Adam hated saying it out loud because it was like some strange personal failing but Coze was here now and he couldn't fail her. Otherwise everything he had ever wanted, built and aspired to would be obliterated and erased from history like every single thing in the Imperium was being.

"I'll take you to the largest impacted area now," Adam said and he walked away before Coze could answer.

He just hoped beyond hope this exploration would get everyone he cared about killed.

***

Adam was seriously surprised how difficult it was to get to the largest impacted area, it might have been on the other side of the planet but for some reason all the workers refused to go there. It also seemed like the machines and shuttles and drones refused to travel there either.

Adam wasn't sure if that had more to do with the drones and other pieces of technology being programmed to only travel to fertile ground, but it was still strange.

After two hours of trying to find a shuttle to take them there, Adam and Coze stepped off the black metal ramp of the circular shuttle and stood on the hard, cracked orange ground.

As the circular shuttle zoomed off into the distance like it was a child running away from a monster, Adam couldn't believe it as he stared out into the distance that stretched on for hundreds of miles, he just couldn't see anything but hard cracked flat land.

This was actually one of the most hilly areas of the planet and that made it perfect for growing grapes, grazing sheep and cows and even creating some genetic hybrids that the Rex said were illegal. Coze didn't need to know that of course.

But now Adam just couldn't believe how an entire farming ecosystem that had been thriving for over twenty years had disappeared overnight and the impacted area was spreading.

The air smelt burnt, crispy and there was a strange undertone of charred flesh that made no sense too.

"What did your workers describe happened?" Coze asked.

Adam shrugged. "They reported working on a hill, picking grapes at night because it's cooler. Then the next moment they were on flat hard, cracked ground with no grapes in their baskets,"

Coze shook her head. "If this is a trick then I swear to you I will kill you,"

Adam shook a few steps away. "Why would I play a trick on you? I didn't even know I supplied the military with food,"

"You don't. At least not yet but the Rex is rearranging how the Imperium's food production works so your planet will become military-only food,"

Adam threw his arms up in the air. "What about all the billions of people that rely on my planet for food? We both know the Rex will not allow them to grow their own food and he will not offer them another Farming World as their source of food,"

Coze grinned. "At least I'm not the only traitor on this planet,"

Adam hardly believed himself to be a traitor to humanity just because he didn't agree with billions of people starving but maybe that was the key to solving this mystery.

Adam knelt down on the hot cracked ground and he was surprised how rough and almost razor sharp the ground was. None of this was natural and he had no idea who would have the technology to actually pull this off.

Except the Rex of course.

Adam looked at Coze. "Why is the Rex killing this planet?"

Coze shrugged. "Because... he isn't. He really isn't trying to kill you or the billions of planets that rely on you. He wants to kill me and my military planet,"

Adam smiled. He hadn't realised that the rumours were true, that the Imperial Army weren't stationed on normal planets and that they were actually stationed on their own planets. Probably some kind of military Fortress Planet.

"Why would he want to kill you?" Adam asked.

Coze looked up at the crystal clear sky for a moment before looking at Adam.

"Because I was wrong to follow the Rex and burn entire planets to the ground. The Rex is wrong and me and my planet have succeeded from the Imperium," she said.

Adam laughed. He had to admit that Lord Commander Coze was extremely ballsy and bold and stupid.

Everyone knew that no one just succeeded from the Imperium without their planet being turned into a wasteland.

"I control two billion soldiers and this entire sector of space," Coze said. "Me turning my back on the Imperium is a massive blow that the Imperium will quickly recover from so me and my forces are fleeing towards the Enlightened Republic,"

Adam laughed. "That's a myth. The Enlightened Republic is simply a myth designed by the Rex to give people false hope,"

Coze grabbed his wrist. "No. It isn't. I encountered a Republic cell operating on my planet and I interrogated them. They showed me proof and they showed me that there was a better way to live,"

Adam wasn't buying it. It was impossible to imagine that there was a group of humans able to live in peace without the constant oversight of the Rex.

"They're a group of solar systems on the furthest reaches of the Imperium that encourage people to learn, vote for democracy and live freely without the control of the Rex,"

Adam waved his hands about. "How does this relate to what's going on on my planet?"

Coze frowned. "The Rex must have learnt that I would come here first before setting off so we would have enough food to make the journey. And I didn't want to burden the Republic when we arrived so I wanted enough food for us to survive for maybe a decade,"

Adam nodded that seemed perfectly reasonable and it was an easy order to fulfil considering he normally sent enough food to last planets twenty or thirty years at a time.

Adam just shook his head as he watched a thin line of dust blew about in the wind and he found it hard to believe that two billion soldiers (a mere drop in the ocean of the Imperium's population and military might) was enough reason to justify destroying an entire Farming World that the Rex knew billions relied on for food.

That was murder to him and Adam had to admit that if the Enlighted Republic did exist then he certainly wanted to be apart of it.

He no longer wanted to live in an Imperium that had such discard for the lives of innocent humans that only wanted to feed themselves, their friends and most importantly their families.

***

Adam stood on an immense circular bridge of a bright white circular warship a few years later and he was just amazed as they entered the Enlightened Republic just how different it was.

They were thousands upon thousands of miles away from the border but the bright red, red and purple planets looked so magical and hopeful that Adam was so looking forward to the future.

He and Coze had become great friends over the past years, and Adam liked to think he had really helped her overcome her past and trauma about burning so many planets to ash. In all fairness she had hardly had a choice and she was only following her conditioning from the Rex.

He was that good at controlling people after all.

The bridge might have been empty with only the gentle hum of the engines keeping him company, but Adam liked how everyone in the fleet was enjoying their evening meals. And whilst he really hoped that the billions of people that relied on Ceres 14 had found another source of food, he still wasn't ashamed that as he, his staff and all of Coze's military lot emptied the planet of food to travel to the Enlightened Republic because it meant that they could help their new friends survive.

And Adam was no military man but he had a feeling that the Rex, his generals and spies were always watching, learning and studying the Enlightened Republic for the right moment to strike and claim it for themselves.

For any degree of peace, freedom or love in the galaxy was just a carefully crafted illusion by the Rex because he wanted humanity all to himself.

And he would never stop until all of humanity worshipped him and he controlled them all, but as long as Adam lived he was going to make sure that never ever happened and if making sure the Enlightened Republic had enough food was a way to do that, then he was perfectly happy with that.

AUTHOR OF AGENTS OF THE EMPEROR SERIES

CONNOR WHITELEY

BATTLE DOCTRINES

A SCIENCE FICTION SPACE OPERA SHORT STORY

BATTLE DOCTRINES

Ship Mistress Olivia Flapper stood on her raised metal platform in the middle of her white spherical bridge on her great warship *Rex's Hammer*. She had always wanted to be a Ship Mistress, a great leader of the Imperium's war efforts and now after so many years of service, fighting and political workings she was finally one of them.

The bridge was still brand-new to Olivia but it was as wonderful as she ever could have imagined. She really liked the spherical shape of the walls, its smooth white metal was a little too shiny in places but she would sort it all out in time.

Her small raised platform was only big enough for her to stand on which was absolutely perfect, especially as Olivia wasn't a fan of the constant smells of body odour, sweat and blood that seemed to pour off her command crew like rain from a duck. It wasn't exactly pleasant.

At least the small bright golden orbs of light bounced around the bridge, bouncing from one wall to another and back again.

Sometimes when Olivia was alone (which wasn't as often as she would have liked) she just stared at the little orbs. Sometimes they were happier, freer and more content with life than she was.

As much as Olivia loved her new position, her service to the Rex and her life, she just felt like there was more to life than always searching for the next promotion and intensely studying the next battle doctrine that old men with no military experience had created.

The circular warship hummed loudly and Olivia looked down at her command crew, all twenty of them, as they were hunched over their large bulky metal computer screens having to have computations by hand, having to calculate their trajectory by hand and having to inform different departments of the warship by hand.

This certainly wasn't the most modern ship she had ever been on but it was customary for all brand-new Ship Masters and Mistresses to get put on the lowest ships first of all. Apparently it was so they could develop their skills, but Olivia knew it was because the new ones were the most likely to die so it was cheaper to put them on poorer ships before "gifting" them the more expensive warships.

She wasn't really a fan of that rule.

Olivia waved at her command crew as they walked about or did their work wearing their long white robes denoting their position and their newness to the role. It was a shame that Olivia was surrounded by newbies judging by their bright white robes without a single speck of dirt on them.

Either they were so new that they had only graduated from the academy in the past two days or the environmental systems were *so* good that they seriously purified the air.

Judging by the rest of the ship, Olivia fully believed it was the former.

"Ship Mistress, we're detecting three enemy ships incoming. Within firing distance in five minutes," a very short man said with a balding head.

Olivia nodded slowly and her hands tightened around the cold metal railings of her raised platform. She had been sent here on this mission to deliver bombs to a faraway planet to help Imperial forces annihilate a rogue cult of Dark Keres, but clearly the enemy didn't want these bombs delivered.

She had no idea what separated the Dark Keres to the rest of their foul, magic freaks of their Keres species. The Treaty of Defeat was such a weak little treaty that might have meant the awful Keres species was starving itself to death but the Dark Keres were awful.

Unlike the normal Keres, these so-called Dark Keres actually had a spine and they were fighting back against the righteousness of humanity. It was humanity's Rex-given right to rule the stars, purge entire species and claim all the planets they wanted.

And it was the Keres's duty to die or at least join humanity as slaves as so many of their foul kind had.

Olivia focused on the icy coldness of space dead away from them as two large holographic screens appeared showing Olivia the endless blackness of space with no nearby planets, imperial forces or stars close by.

They were alone.

Olivia really didn't want to fight these Dark Keres because they might have been breaking the law time after time but they were just trying to do what they could to survive.

Humanity was constantly doing questionable things to make sure it survived, so maybe the Keres' weren't so different from them after all.

"Battle Doctrine Mistress," a very tall woman said.

Olivia bit her lip as she couldn't even see the foul enemy ships yet, she didn't know what Dark Keres ships looked like but she was going to have to proceed as her training suggested she should.

"Advancement Battle Doctrine," Olivia said.

As the bridge became a hive of activity with her command crew running round like headless chickens, she had to admit it wasn't her favourite Doctrine.

The Advancement Doctrine was sadly all about travelling quickly through space to make sure the enemy couldn't catch up with them. It meant deactivating the weapon systems to give the engines more power but hopefully it would still work.

Olivia really wanted to see the enemy but she just couldn't.

The Keres were masters of their magic and it was so damn

annoying that they were probably using it to cloak their ships. For all Olivia knew they could be right next to them.

"How did you know the Keres were here in the first place?" Olivia asked.

None of the command crew were paying attention to her as the warship hummed, banged and vibrated as the engines were given more power. She hated this.

Olivia had fought the Keres plenty of times and whilst the Dark Keres might be different to the rest of their race, she was still willing to bet that they used the same or similar tactics.

The Keres were waiting to ambush them and she feared that the Advancement Doctrine was exactly what they wanted.

"We found them on the edge of the system for a brief second before they cloaked themselves," a woman said as she rushed past.

Olivia nodded but it made no sense. The Keres knew that they couldn't outgun, beat or destroy an Imperial warship because they were so weak, so why in the Rex's fine name did they reveal themselves?

Unless it was all part of a plan.

It was moments like this that just made Olivia want to jump into Ultraspace and zoom through the galaxy at light speed regardless of how apparently dangerous that was with the bombs.

She just wanted to keep her crew alive, and herself of course.

"Scan the surrounding area," Olivia said.

Only one man looked up at her but he shrugged as he ran the scan and then shook his head at her.

Olivia's heart pounded in her chest. She was used to dealing with impossible humans, impossible tasks and impossible crew members. She wasn't used to dealing with impossible aliens.

She didn't want her crew to die. She didn't want to fail. She had to deliver the bombs to the planet over ten hours away.

Then Olivia realised that sometimes the Keres did a little trick where they magically project their ships into space to make the Imperium believe they were in one location when they were actually in another.

The enemy was a lot closer than Olivia ever wanted to admit.

Then Olivia felt her skin turn icy cold and she had only ever had that reaction once. Seconds before the Keres attacked her in the most violent way possible.

"Invasion Doctrine!" Olivia shouted.

But it was too late.

The ship jerked.

Throwing Olivia across the bridge.

Other crew members smashed around her.

Bodies shattering.

Streaks of blood painting the walls.

Alarms screamed overhead.

Flashing lights exploded on.

Olivia forced herself up. She forced herself towards her raised platform.

Her body screamed in protest but she accessed her private hologram.

She saw thousands of victims all over the ship from the impact. A bomb had hit their starboard side but their shields were intact and their anti-magic systems were okay.

At least the Keres couldn't teleport or board them for now.

The two massive holograms that showed her the darkness of space earlier now showed three immense dagger-like warships with blood red crystal hulls appear next to her.

Olivia couldn't believe that the damn Dark Keres were right next to them. That was the last thing she wanted.

She had to somehow figure out a way to keep herself and her crew alive and how to get the bombs to the battlefleet.

For the briefest of moments Olivia supposed she could activate the bombs right now and just kill them all and the Keres warships next to her. But she didn't want to use the No Hope Doctrine just yet.

She wouldn't dare give the alien abominations some reward for their attack. Olivia was going to win no matter what it took.

"Mistress," a voice said but Olivia didn't bother to see who it was. "The Keres want to contact us. They're requesting we surrender to them,"

Olivia shook her head. These damn aliens were never going to get her to surrender.

Olivia forced herself upright and she gripped the metal railings of her raised platform and frowned at the two holographic screens showing the enemy warships.

"We need to activate the weapon systems immediately," Olivia said.

"It will do us no good. The enemy are on the starboard side and our weapons on that side are destroyed," a man said.

Olivia couldn't believe how damn infuriating these aliens were. And the man was right sadly.

A loud humming of pure magical energy crackled around her and Olivia rolled her eyes as the damn anti-magic systems were failing. It wouldn't be too long now until the Keres invaded and slaughtered them all like the beasts they were.

Olivia opened a ship-wide communication channel. "All forces this is the Ship Mistress enact the Containment Doctrine immediately. Do not allow a witch to live,"

Olivia just shook her head even more as her command crew all bit their lower lip. They all knew this was bad because if the anti-magic generators collapsed then the Keres would easily rip into reality and stalk the holy halls of their warship.

And they would kill human after human until they all died.

The Containment Doctrine was simple but useless. A simple hell mary to throw into the air to buy Olivia some more time.

"What about the engines?" Olivia asked.

A young woman from the crew stepped forward. "Contained by Keres. They're using our magic to immobilise them. I could undo the magic but it would take time,"

"How much?"

"Ten minutes," she said.

The air crackled and murderous screams echoed around the ship.

"Do it," Olivia said to the woman before turning to her crew. "Connect me to Keres ships. I'll buy us some time. Weapons won't free us here. Words might,"

Olivia could literally feel the tension in the bridge now and she wanted to slice it with a sword but she had to focus and remain strong. Some Keres creatures only needed eye contact to use their magic.

Olivia had to focus and not allow the abominations to use their magic on her.

Moments later a very tall, thin elf-like woman appeared in blue holographic form with very long golden black hair that flowed around her like angelic wings.

"You must hand over your weapons please my friend," the woman said. "My forces want to unleash their Death Magic on you but I am buying you time,"

Olivia grinned. The woman's voice was very elegant, lyrical and perfect but she was just stupid. Olivia was a Ship Mistress of the Imperium, she did not listen to the lies and deceits and corruption that aliens spread.

And she wasn't going to give them anything.

As soon as the engines were free once more she was going to escape and jump into Ultraspace and to hell with the consequences.

"I will not give you a damn thing alien. These bombs will reach the planet and they will be dropped on your kind and then humanity will rule the stars," Olivia said.

She wasn't exactly sure if she believed it and she didn't know if the Keres on the planet deserved to die but she wanted to act tough at least.

Olivia noticed the female Keres was looking at someone else probably behind the hologram then the female Keres nodded.

"Then you leave me no choice and I know your workers are trying to free the engines," she said.

The entire command crew went still but Olivia waved them to continue.

"Let me show you just a touch of our Death Magic," the woman said before uttering strange twisted words in a tongue Olivia didn't understand or care to listen to.

Olivia cut the transmission but when she looked back at her command crew they were all wide-eyed with terror as they stared back at their computer screens.

Olivia climbed down and looked at the silent ghostly pictures of their friends, fellow crew members and even loved ones turn to black crystal before shattering into dust.

"Two percent of the crew is dead," someone said but Olivia didn't care who.

"Are the engines free?" Olivia asked.

"Almost," a woman said.

Olivia climbed back up to her raised platform and contacted the Keres warships again.

"Did you like my gift? I know the Goddess of Souls was particularly happy," the female Keres said.

Olivia's hands formed fists. She seriously didn't care for the strange alien mythology of the Keres.

The air charged with magic energy and Olivia felt the icy coldness of the Keres's foul touch around her. They were within striking distance.

She just had to buy her crew a little more time.

"Does your Goddess love Keres souls?" Olivia asked.

The female Keres laughed. "Souls are souls my dear. I'll let you meet her now. Because now you die!"

An alien claw formed in the air.

Slashing at Olivia.

She stumbled back.

The claw chased her.

Olivia leapt off her platform.

She smashed onto the floor.

The claw lashed at her.

Olivia rolled forward.

Another claw appeared in front of her.

Olivia jumped to one side.

She hit a table.

The two claws flew at her.

The ship jerked.

The engines were free.

"Into Ultraspace!" Olivia shouted.

The entire ship screamed in protest.

The Keres were trying to anchor them into reality.

Olivia whipped out her pistol.

She shot the two claws.

They disappeared.

The warship zoomed off into Ultraspace and all Olivia could think about was how badly she didn't want the bombs to explode.

***

Olivia absolutely had to admit that the next hour was the longest one of her entire life, each second she was half-expecting one of her crew to shout that the bombs were overheating or somehow having a reaction to Ultraspace travel.

Thankfully they weren't.

Olivia just smiled as she leant against the warm metal railings of her raised platform and watched as the streaks of purple light from the Ultraspace network tunnel (she really didn't know how it worked) zoomed past her.

Then with a quiet thud the tunnel disappeared and Olivia was so damn happy that she was alive and that her crew were okay. Then the entire ship hummed a little as an Imperial network connected to her ship and took control of the bombs.

For a small moment Olivia thought that the Dark Keres had followed her but everyone knew that the Keres were too dumb to use Ultraspace and they stuck with their clearly inferior Nexus System of their own magical creation.

Olivia didn't know how it worked and she didn't want to know. The Keres were dumb, end of story.

And as she watched on the two massive holograms the Imperial fleet zooming around an orange green planet with Keres ships trying to flee, she grinned as the bombs rushed towards the planet ready to be used exactly where they were needed most.

Olivia still wasn't sure if this was just, needed or even right but she hadn't examined the facts of the battle and in all fairness it hadn't mattered.

As much as she didn't like to admit it, the military wasn't designed to produce thinkers, it was designed to produce soldiers that could pick up a gun and march to the beat of the Rex's eternal war machine so humanity could be kept safe, secured and all the enemies could be killed.

The laughter, cheering and even some happy dances filled the bridge as the command crew and everyone else on the ship was so happy to be alive and Olivia was definitely going to join them later on.

She might have doomed a lot of aliens to death but she had helped to protect humanity, her crew and the future of the Imperium. That was certainly a job very well.

And with thousands of other battlefields spread out across the galaxy, Olivia was really excited about flying away from here and seeing what other great adventures, herself, her crew and her great lower warship could travel to.

Then maybe, just maybe Olivia could finally get a promotion and get a real warship because as she had survived this adventure Olivia was fairly sure she could survive anything.

And that was a great realisation to have and that was all thanks to her battle doctrines.

AUTHOR OF AGENTS OF THE EMPEROR SERIES

CONNOR WHITELEY

COMMUNICATING IN ULTRASPACE

A SCIENCE FICTION SPACE OPERA SHORT STORY

COMMUNICATING IN ULTRASPACE

This was the day he died.

Chief Communication Officer Grayson Jones sat on a large grey metal table that was surprisingly smooth, shiny and very relaxing oddly enough. It was almost strange for a table in his little metal boxroom of a break room to be so relaxing and well-maintained. Normally when he worked on ships the breakrooms were so dilapidated that they were just flat out disgusting.

Thankfully everything about the brand-new black circular ship imaginatively called the *Communication* was up to date, clean and perfectly maintained. Grayson had already been on the ship for two weeks and he had yet to find a single problem with the ship.

The only problem with the ship was that it was the smooth walls of the break room were just so plain and dull. Grayson wanted to splash some colour on the walls and maybe hang a few pictures. A nice red, blue or orange might have looked nice and it would be a nice reminder of his homeworld.

Grayson really liked that idea as he wrapped his rough hand around his coffee mug, the sharp bitter taste of it was one of the highlights of living on the ships. And it helped to provide a brief distraction against the overwhelming aromas of roasted peaches, sweat and salted peanuts that clung to everything in the corridor amongst the ship.

He didn't know why the environmental systems were so obsessed with the smell, they could have been faulty, but it was rather nice at first before getting old real quick.

At least the job was simple enough, he was just in charge of making sure all the equipment ran smoothly so all the nearby Imperial forces could route their communications through his station, before the ship blasted the messages off through Ultraspace towards their destination.

Ultraspace was amazing and Grayson really loved learning about it at university. It was just stunning how humanity had managed to create or tap into an intergalactic network of tunnels that allowed for faster-than-light travel.

It was simply brilliant.

And the only thing Grayson needed to do was keep it all working otherwise he absolutely hated to imagine what would happen if he failed. Battle orders might not be read or sent, distress calls might not be heard and vital intelligence might not be known about aliens and terrorists.

If Grayson failed then he sadly knew a lot of good people could die and there was no way he was ever allowing himself to have that on his conscious. He didn't volunteer for five years in the Peace Corps to allow innocent people to die.

"We have a problem," a woman said as a large circular door opened with an annoying screaming sound that almost made Grayson jump.

He looked at the Chief of Engineering, a beautiful woman called Mary wearing a very attractive pink blouse, trousers and white trainers.

But if she was coming to him then it had to be bad.

"What happened this time?" Grayson asked grinning.

"The Ultraspace generator died," Mary said plainly.

Grayson just shook his head. Of all the damn things that could possibly go wrong, he seriously didn't want this to be the problem.

Without their Ultraspace generator then the ship couldn't run away or travel through the network basically increasing their travel time by a factor of 100 and that meant the Ultraspace Communicator would fail sooner or later too.

Grayson had sadly worked too many jobs where the failing of the Ultraspace generator wasn't seen as the first sign of an Ultraspace shutdown on the ship so when the damn aliens attacked. There was no way of escape or call for help.

Those people always died.

"And there's ten Keres ships two systems over. The great benefits of invading their territory," Mary said.

Grayson seriously didn't want to attract the attention of the foul alien beasts with their awful magic. He wanted to escape in short order and he hardly agreed with Mary about space being the Keres' domain. The stars belonged to humanity and only humanity.

"I presume you've tried turning it on and off?" Grayson asked.

Mary playfully hit him over the head. "I didn't come to you to get mocked. This is a communicator error, the Ultraspace Communicator is *telling* the Generator to shut down,"

Grayson leant forward. He had heard a hell of a lot of things in his decades of service as a soldier fighting the Keres and then even more as a communication specialist. He had never heard of pieces of the ship *telling* each other what to do.

He wasn't even sure if the Keres's magic could do such things to Imperial ships.

"Take me there immediately please," Grayson said.

He was surprised at how hesitant Mary was to let him go but she nodded after a few seconds and smiled.

"You're going to need an environmental suit. It's pretty nasty in there,"

Grayson hated it how his stomach twisted into a painful knot as he realised that things were going to get a hell of a lot worse before they could ever get better.

***

Grayson had always hated damn environmental suits. He hated their bright red appearance that made him look like a tomato, he hated how his movements were so slow and controlled and he hated how it was always just damn impossible to see out of them.

Even now as he slowly went into the environmentally sealed Ultraspace chamber, an immense black metal chamber with two huge metal tanks containing strange complex technology allowing them to tap into Ultraspace whenever they wanted, Grayson realised just how bad this all actually was.

He had been in chambers like this all over the Imperium and they never changed much but they were always clean, smelt sweet and they always left the taste of lemon drizzle cake on his tongue just like how his father used to make it when he was a child.

But this chamber was simply disgusting with the smell and taste of harsh chemicals, toxic radiation and death filling his senses. His suit's warning systems were already starting to flare to life and no one else knew this but Grayson knew there was a rip in Ultraspace.

He had read about Ultraspace rips plenty of times and they were always kept under wraps and a strange type of radiation always leaked into the ships and sometimes something worse leaked through with them.

He didn't know what the reports said about the so-called creatures that leaked through the rips but people died and then became ghosts of a fashion. Grayson had no intention of dying today so he looked around for a weapon but there weren't any.

He had thought he was going to die plenty of times in battle, on ships or getting involved in beer brawls. Normally he didn't care about dying as long as it was in service but for some reason he just felt closer to Death than even before.

As Grayson went towards the two metal tanks he could have sworn that he heard laughter and people wanting him to do something. It was like a corrupting chant in the back of his mind urging him to do something dangerous.

He felt the urge to remove his helmet so he could breathe more freely and not have to listen to the constant groan of his breathing but he couldn't.

He had to stay alive or everyone else on the ship might die too.

Grayson took out a smaller scanner that he had picked up on the way over here and he started scanning the chamber and surprisingly enough the Ultraspace Generator was working perfectly.

In fact, everything was apparently working perfectly, or it was working well enough not to register.

Grayson looked at Mary and just frowned as she had completely removed her environmental suit, her eyes had sunken in on themselves and her feet were now ghostly.

He shook his head as he realised that the rip had corrupted her and she had come to get him because he was the only one that could stop the corruption.

"Death is the ruler of the Network not humanity," Mary said. "Humanity might have wiped out my creations of the Keres but we will rise again,"

Grayson broke out into a fighting position. He had no idea what the hell had corrupted Mary but it was clearly insane.

Sure humanity wanted to obliterate the aliens but they weren't dead yet sadly. So this corrupting creature had to be something to do with their strange alien mythology and abominable magic.

This creature had to die.

The creature infecting Mary just grinned and kept looking at him up and down like he was a piece of meat ready for the slaughter.

Grayson tried to think harder about what had happened to the surviving members of the ships where rips had occurred. He couldn't remember. He knew he had to close the rip but he didn't know how.

He didn't even know how the rips occurred in the first place.

"I see your mind human. You fear me. And just know that Death grows stronger so your Network will die like your race,"

Mary charged.

Her fingers became swords.

She slashed them.

Grayson rolled to one side.

He couldn't move.

His suit wasn't flexible enough.

He was stuck.

He felt Mary slashed his back.

Grayson screamed as radiation poured into him.

His lungs roared as toxic chemicals filled them.

He screamed as his body turned cancerous.

Every single cell felt like it was fire and then his world went black.

But he knew that he had died for sure.

***

Grayson hated how ghostly, light and strange he felt as he woke up on the bright white floor of an Ultraspace Tunnel. It felt so weird to be inside a tunnel and yet not blinded by its intense white sterile light with a few white circular ships zooming overhead.

The air was unfortunately cold, icy and bitter and Grayson really didn't like how the air smelt of damp, but he just couldn't understand why he was inside a tunnel and not dead-dead.

He looked down at his legs, arms and chest and he bit his lip as he realised that he was like a ghost. He wasn't completely see-through but he might as well have been.

When he turned around Grayson shook his head as he saw a tear the size of his hand behind him, he went out to touch it but crippling pain filled him. He knew that the rip lead to his ship but he was dead so he could never return.

A strange suckling and humming and buzzing sound came from behind him.

Grayson turned around and he wanted to swear as he saw a very thin shadowy black figure like the Grim Reaper carrying his scythes that Grayson just knew was dripping his own blood.

The figure didn't smile or anything, or maybe he was because Grayson couldn't see his face but the figure was immensely tall, easily five times the height of him. And yet Grayson had no idea what he was.

"I told you I get more and more powerful each day human," the figure said.

"What are you?" Grayson asked. "I don't know you. I don't know who you are. You are nothing to me,"

Grayson guessed that made the Figure smile.

"I am one of the Gods that you claim don't exist. The Keres called me The Destroyer but I prefer the term The Obliterator. Now you have served in your military. You know what I can do?"

Grayson looked to the bright white floor for a moment and he did sort of remember the strange heretical beliefs of the Keres. They believed in a Dark and Light group of gods with The Destroyer being the creator of their Death Magic but they were just myths.

Myths created by a strange doomed dying pathetic race of aliens that humanity would hopefully slaughter one day.

The figure echoed. "Humans are so stupid. You doubt I exist but I feed on your thoughts, your dreams, your ambitions every single time you travel through my network. Do you think it was an accident that your Rex found the Network?"

Grayson nodded.

"Of course not. I grow stronger with more of my Dark Gods are being found and soon I will be free of this prison and soon the galaxy shall burn once again with my rage,"

"Again?" Grayson asked.

The Figure laughed even more. "It is amazing humans can even begin to imagine the grandeur and complexities of the galaxy but I will not tell you anymore. So how about we make a deal?"

Grayson really didn't know what to do about this figure, he was clearly evil, deranged and hellbent on destroying humanity but he could also be a weapon against the Keres. And any weapon against the Keres was a good friend to Grayson.

"Whatever you want," Grayson said.

The Figure laughed as he stretched out a palm without fingers and black energy shot out of them.

The tendrils of black magic swirled, twirled and whirled around Grayson and he screamed in agony for a brief moment as the magic turned him to ash.

But whilst he knew that humanity was ultimately doomed if they didn't learn how to work with the Keres instead of facing them because of the sheer power of the servants of The Destroyer, he knew that his life, knowledge and power was being exchanged for sealing up the rip.

So his friends, crew and ship were now safe and Grayson smiled as he finally became just another white light in the tunnels because he had done his mission, and that would have to be enough for now.

And at least he died in service. Just like he always wanted.

AUTHOR OF AGENTS OF THE EMPEROR SERIES

CONNOR WHITELEY

BLACKHEART
A SCIENCE FICTION FAR FUTURE SHORT STORY

BLACKHEART

Brother meets brother.

Being Imperial Regent has a hell of a lot of great, amazing and rather delightful benefits that I, Jack Blackheart, certainly enjoy most of the time. Especially, as I stood on the very top of the immense black metal Imperial Fortress with the icy cold wing slowly rubbing my cheeks dry.

I had always enjoyed the Fortress way too much actually. It was such a beacon of the Rex's immense power, authority and sheer brutality with its huge black 8-point star design that stretched on for thousands of miles in all directions and upwards even more.

It was next to impossible to look down below and see the charred black stone ground that so many soldiers walked over every day, because it was their duty to the Rex. I actually wanted to know if they did this out of choice but I doubted I could ever get a reliable answer.

The part of the fortress I was standing on had to be my favourite. I was north towards the largest city on Earth and it might have been miles upon miles away but it still looked great with its fiery spires reaching up into space and so many little beautiful lights of ships, shuttles and fighters buzzing around the city like bees.

The wind might have been icy cold scented with wonderful hints of jasmine, lavender and peanuts leaving the good taste of nature on my tongue but I honestly could have stayed out here for hours.

And that city was so damn beautiful.

On cold dark nights like this, it was something to behold and it just reminded me how great humanity could be. When I first joined the Rex, I was so filled with hope about the Imperium.

Of course back then I believe, I believed the Imperium was a force for good, change and the betterment of everyone. But that was a lie, probably the biggest lie in human history because the Imperium was all about control these days.

I was probably the most free person in the Imperium because I was the Rex's right and left hand but even I felt the imposing stare of security cameras from time to time. So I just admired the sheer beauty of the nearby city and just dreamed for a single moment that the people in the city might be free, laughing and smiling with each other.

Footsteps came up behind me and I dared to imagine it was someone to save me.

I just had to smile at that idea because whenever I visited a place in the Imperium, I always donated Rexes, food and machinery to the local population just so they might have a better life, and maybe I could continue to believe in that small, small moment that the Imperium was a force for good once again.

I often argued with myself about leaving, running away and just abandoning the Rex to his crazy delusions of control and power but I didn't want to.

As stupid as it sounded this was still my home, the Rex had found me when I was a late teenager on the streets and starving so he bought me in, gave me food and shelter.

And I served him, happily at first and now I just press on because the work can be great at times.

"You're up late tonight, Lord Regent,"

I recognised the voice instantly. It was a deep female voice so I turned around and grinned at my old friend Perrigin, or Perry for short, in a great-looking blue dress, military boots and small gun in her hand. She still looked beautiful.

She was meant to be in charge of forcing the various Planetary

Governors in the Imperium to the Rex's Will but she was so good at it that most of them didn't notice they were being manipulated. And most of the time Perry was just too much fun to be around.

But she looked serious tonight.

"I never knew you had a brother," Perry said not daring to look at me.

I frowned at her. I hadn't even thought of my brother for four decades, he had abandoned me when the Rex's forces invaded our settlement and killed our parents. It was the reason why I was on the streets and it was awful.

My brother had been a good man, a hard worker and a good fighter but whilst all the other men and women in our settlement rushed to fight the invaders. My brother ran. I screamed out his name. He ran even faster.

"Why?" I asked.

Perry shrugged. "I have a new prisoner to enjoy and he claims to be your brother,"

I had to nod at that. It was a hell of a story and I still didn't understand why the Rex "gifted" prisoners to Perry. I know that her mother was an expert interrogator but I doubted she had passed on the knowledge to Perry.

"You want me to talk to him then?" I asked, really hoping she would say no so I could continue to enjoy the view.

"Yes because if this is your brother then I want to know why he was sneaking about trying to assassinate the Rex," Perry said frowning.

A lump caught in my throat as I realised that if this was truly my brother then he was a dead man. As much as I too wanted the Rex dead, I certainly wasn't stupid enough to try.

He was too smart, too well protected and too damn paranoid to ever allow an assassin within two miles of him. Let alone allow an assassin into his Fortress.

"Take me to him," I said.

Perry hugged me, grabbed me by the hand and she dragged me

towards the prisoner.

This wasn't going to end well I knew that for sure.

***

One of the many foundational lies the Imperium is built on is that the Imperium is a type of democracy where the millions upon millions of planetary governors vote amongst themselves for who should have critical roles. Like the people in charge of the military, policing, security and so on.

It's all a lie because the Rex controls everything and every single bit of freedom a person believes they have is a carefully crafted lie by the Rex himself.

I was starting to understand that now.

I followed Perry into a massive stone domed chamber with rough grey walls and it was barely large enough to swing a cat inside, and as soon as I stepped inside the temperature dropped so much my breath formed thick columns of vapour.

It was a horrible feeling seeing the hairs on my arms shoot up like defences and small crystals of ice formed on me. The chamber looked like it was meant to be warm and cosy but nothing could be further from the truth.

There were no white-armoured guards or soldiers in the chamber like I had seen in their thousands all over the Fortress. There was only a single man in the chamber with his cheeks and eyes swollen so much that I couldn't tell if this was my brother or not.

Sure the man had the same long raven black hair as my brother but it was burnt and ripped out in places, probably thanks to Perry.

The man's fingers were bleeding and shooting off in weird angles and I really didn't care to look at the rest of him.

I didn't have a cast-iron stomach like Perry clearly did.

My stomach twisted into a painful knot just looking at him so I focused on a small chipped spot on the domed wall behind him instead.

"You came then," he said in a course loving voice that my brother always used on me because he really did love me back in the day.

The lump from earlier returned stronger to my throat. I just couldn't believe this was my brother. The big brother that had taught me how to hack into a holo-system. The big brother that had cooked my dinners when our parents had to work late. The big brother that had loved me every moment of every day.

He was here and he was suffering.

"I came because it is my duty to the Rex," I said out of instinct.

My brother grinned. "Do you remember my name brother?"

I nodded. "Jason,"

Perry smiled as she took out a massive dagger. "This dagger is way too clean for my liking so please tell me, who are you working for?"

I forced myself not to look in horror at my friend. She shouldn't be doing this, this was wrong on so many levels.

"I would rather die than tell you Rex scum," Jason said.

Perry laughed. She went to thrust the dagger into him but I grabbed her wrist.

Her eyes widened as we both realised what the hell I had just done and I seriously hoped that Perry was going to break her orders and training by not killing me immediately.

"I will get the information from him," I said hoping to buy myself some time. "If he still doesn't give me the information then you can flay him alive if you care,"

I didn't want that to happen but I wanted more time.

Perry nodded so I went down and knelt in front of my brother's twisted tortured form.

"Did you ever find a boyfriend?" I asked smiling. That was actually what I hoped had happened to him over the years, I hoped my big brother had found love, happiness and joy.

He frowned and looked at Perry. "She killed him two years ago,"

I nodded. "I'm sorry,"

At least that ruled out any romantic links being the people helping him but I didn't know what I was hoping to achieve by getting the information from him.

He was going to die unless I could magically come up with an idea to save the both of us. I was clever. I just doubted I was that clever.

"I won't tell you who's helping me," Jason said.

"But they'll kill you if you don't,"

"They're going to kill me anyway," he said and I knew he was lying.

"Then I can promise you they'll kill you faster and less painfully," I said looking at Perry.

She rolled her eyes like I had just taken the fun out of her playtime but she nodded.

I was about to take Jason's hands but then I realised how mutilated they were and how tortured the rest of his body was. I didn't dare touch him in case it caused him crippling pain.

"Please. You protected me a lot during school and my childhood. Let me repay the favour by helping you now," I said.

He shook his head. "Why do you work for them?"

And before I realised it I was replying out of instinct. "Because the Rex is the only one that can help humanity not descend into chaos, hatred and anarchy. He is the difference between freedom and chaos and control and safety,"

Jason laughed. "I will not tell you who helped me because there was no one. I don't work with the Keres and their magic, I don't work with the Enlightened Republic and I don't work with anyone else,"

I almost believed him because humanity hated the foul alien Keres with their freakish magic with a passion. I had met people from the independent and so-called free people of the Enlightened Republic and my brother didn't have the arrogance of them, but my brother had lied.

He had admitted he worked with people because Perry had killed his boyfriend two years ago.

"You worked with your boyfriend so who are you working

with?" I asked. "I am Imperial Regent, I designed and reviewed the security plans of this Fortress myself almost daily. Unless you had inside help, it is impossible for you to do this,"

Then I looked at Perry and I frowned.

I reached for a weapon I normally carried but I was having it cleaned tonight as I was meeting the Rex tomorrow.

When I looked at Perry again she had a dagger pointed at me and I just shook my head. She was a traitorous bastard and then she clicked her fingers.

Jason screamed in agony as his bones, muscles and skin were ripped apart and reforged into the image of Jason's real form. He was tall, muscular and attractive like a university jock that all the girls gushed over. He looked perfect.

But I just couldn't believe that Perry had magic or something. I knew as Imperial Regent that it was a lie that no human could produce magic but the numbers were like 1 in every one trillion.

I had no idea that Perry had magic before now.

"So why this?" I asked.

"Because I knew you were a fake," Jason said. "My brother was a good man, he hated the Rex and he never would have attacked a woman trying to help me kill him. You have changed. You are one of his puppets,"

I shook my head and noticed there was a small red flashing light behind them and I sort of felt like I needed to make them confess.

It was a strange sensation but as soon as I thought about it I realised I was right. Yet if there was help coming to stop these assassins then I just wanted to make sure I didn't die in the process.

And the Rex's help was always conditional on me being loyal to him. If I showed any sign of weakness here then he would allow these two to kill me.

Before killing them himself.

"This isn't delusion Jason. This is just the truth. The truth is the Rex is the only person who could save humanity and that's a good person," I said not even forcing out the words.

Jason took a dagger out from his back. "I'm disappointed that you allowed yourself to believe in these lies,"

I shook my head. I had to find out what their plan was.

"And why you Perry?" I asked. "You were always good to the Rex and he rewarded you,"

"Because everything is a lie and everything will burn!" Perry shouted.

She charged at me.

I jumped back.

She swung again.

I punched her.

Jason tackled me.

Pinning me against the wall.

He whacked me round the face.

Forcing his blade against my throat.

"Why do this?" I asked. "What do you intend to achieve? Make us a democratic republic?"

"I would never allow us to become like the Enlightened Republic but Truth must happen," Perry said.

And then I realised exactly what had happened to her. My good friend Perry had simply allowed herself to think too much about reality, she questioned all the lies and propaganda and the foundations the Imperium was built on.

As Imperial Regent I often created the foundational lies and considered them, it was possible to know what was fact and what was fiction these days but reality was a lie.

Of course over the years it had destroyed my mental health, I had been on the brink so many times of just wanting to annihilate it all because I just wanted the truth.

I had never jumped off the edge. Clearly Perry had.

I looked my brother dead in the eye. He didn't want to do this. He looked vulnerable.

I punched him.

He fell backwards.

I jumped forward.

Grabbing the dagger.

Snatching it out of his hand.

He charged at me.

I thrusted the blade into his chest.

Perry charged at me.

Screaming in emotional agony.

She wasn't focusing.

She swung her blade.

I ducked.

She rushed past me.

I leapt up.

Stabbing her in the back.

And as the Rex's personal white-armoured bodyguards stormed in, I just shook my head as I stared at the corpse of my dear big brother and I truly realised that these two were always going to die tonight.

Because every single freedom a person thought they had was a simple lie created by the Rex.

This was all a test and one I feared for my life that I had passed. I hoped.

***

The next morning I was standing at my most favourite spot on the immense stone fortress walls staring at the beautiful city in the distance. The bright morning was surprisingly warm, calm and the sun was strongly beaming down on me like a spotlight. The air was wonderfully fresh with hints of jasmine, lavender and pecans filling the air and I was so glad to be alive.

Last night might as well have been a blur for all the good that happened to me. The bodyguards had stormed in and chopped up the corpses to make sure my dear brother and Perry were well and truly dead and then the chunks were taken away.

I was left alone in the room for a few moments before I confidently walked out and I almost jumped out of my own skin at the imposing sight of the Rex in his jet-black, twisted, terrifying armour.

He didn't say anything to me. He only grinned, smiled and nodded like he had been proven right about me and maybe he had.

I had always believed that I was different to the rest of the Fortress, I believed that I was playing a long game against the Rex but maybe I wasn't anything that I thought I was. Maybe I really had become the lies, deceit and carefully crafted mould of what I was meant to be by the Rex's design.

And now I was thinking about it, maybe that wasn't a bad thing. Sure the Rex was a master of manipulation but he trusted me, wanted me to live and I was already the second most powerful person in the entire Imperium so maybe, just maybe I should start acting like it.

Of course I wouldn't take the galaxy for myself but maybe I could have all the power I desired and I could become something, someone completely different to the little boy who had lost his brother and parents.

Maybe I could become something far greater but simply allowing the Rex to remain in power for a little while longer, because there was a simple truth that everyone, even people as *smart* as the Rex, forgets and that is that every ruler falls in the end.

Every King, Emperor and Regent in human history has fallen at some point and when one of them falls there is something, someone to replace them.

And I'm fully determined to make sure when the Rex falls that I am the person to replace him and history will remember my name and there is a single word that will echo across the centuries as the person who took over the Imperium after the evil Rex had fallen.

I just smiled and allowed the warm sun to embrace me lovingly as I realised just how great the future could be, and I was really looking forward to how everyone would remember the simple name *Blackheart* in the bitter end.

AUTHOR OF AGENTS OF THE EMPEROR SERIES

CONNOR WHITELEY

DYING IN SPACE

A SCIENCE FICTION SPACE OPERA SHORT STORY

DYING IN SPACE

No fuel. No power. No environmental systems.

Well, this was a massive clusterfuck if there was ever was one, and I mean I have been in some serious scraps at times. From me escaping Justices before they killed me for crimes I didn't commit, me having to escape from brainwashing camps because the so-called Rex didn't believe I was worshipping him enough and me having to stitch up my infected laser wounds from stupid Imperial Soldiers shooting at me.

I was very well known to pain, agony and annoying people unfortunately.

But even I have to admit that this might actually be my final trip in the Imperium because I sit on the icy cold black metal floor of my bridge, just a posh name for a small circular disc on top of my circular shuttle with a few ugly grey consoles and a broken metal throne on it. That throne was meant to be where I commanded the shuttle from but it was broken.

So the controls were broken.

Three bright flashes lit up the void in the distance.

I'd been on this damn shuttle for days now, cruising past bright fiery white stars that shone like mocking beacons of hope as my misery only grew, and now I was well and truly fucked.

I was nothing more than a mere floating shard of metal flying through the pitch darkness of space without any planets, help or humans nearby.

Part of me wondered if I actually would have liked some company, I hated the idea of dying alone and forgotten but I suppose that's just my large human ego that pops up from time to time. And true to behold, having other people here might just get me killed, so I had to be alone.

The silence of the shuttle was deafening and I seriously wasn't a fan of the silence. For the past few months I had been listening to the constant hum, pop and bang of various systems keeping the shuttle working perfectly, so the silence was just creepy.

Even the air was strange now with its delightfully sweet aromas of basil, tomatoes and garlic from my dinners being replaced with burnt oil and burnt flesh. I really didn't want to know what on Earth had been cooked in the engines.

Three huge flashes appeared at the corner of my eye.

My engines were completely dead, my environmental systems weren't recycling oxygen anymore and even the emergency power of the ship wasn't working.

Thankfully I somehow had some anti-gravity left over but even that seemed to be failing slowly so I was seriously running out of time to somehow get rescued. Or I would die.

I supposed I could have called in Imperial Rescue but even though they pretended to be an independent organisation from the Rex and his Imperial Government, everyone knew they were working for him directly. As soon as I notified them, they would send warships to my location and I would be slaughtered.

You might be wondering what I possibly could have done to piss off the Imperium so much?

And I will most certainly tell you my good man (or woman), I simply questioned the Imperium. You see ever since humanity crawled out of the oceans, developed limbs to become apes and then evolve into humans, they have always learnt.

I wanted to learn about the wider galaxy so I studied astrophysics at the University of Earth, one of the top universities in the Imperium but it was also one of the most censored by the Rex.

A lot of my classmates didn't realise that whilst our lectures, assignments and textbooks were long, they were very skilfully crafted to make us *seem* like we were learning tons but we actually weren't. We weren't being taught anything that the Rex perceived to be forbidden knowledge and the Rex loved people to believe that all knowledge was bad knowledge.

In reality if humanity was dumb then it made them a lot more compliant with whatever he wanted to do.

So I setup out to learn more about the galaxy, the Rex found out and now he was hunting me because I had learnt more about the galaxy in two weeks than I had learnt in four years of my undergraduate degree. That was how controlling the Rex was.

A flash appeared outside.

I stood up and forced my breathing to remain level as I was very conscious about the lack of oxygen in the bridge and I didn't dare waste a single gram of it. I really wanted to be saved but this was a very dodgy part of the Imperium.

I peered out into the pitch darkness of space and whilst there were no planets nearby I did notice a large black cube outside.

The cube itself was pitch black, perfectly smooth and about the size of a human's head. I could only see it because of the reflection off a distant star.

I wanted to reach out and touch it but I couldn't because of my bridge's windows and I knew it was most probably dangerous.

One cube became three cubes.

I had backed away from the windows and I just shook my head in disbelief. I had no idea where the other two cubes came from but this was serious now.

Metal cubes didn't just appear out of nowhere and given how I was still in the Imperium I was willing to bet that these were sensory drones belonging to pirates, aliens or the Imperium.

Pirates would simply smash up my ship and make me a slave. The foul alien Keres would probably savage my ship and use their corrupting magic to turn me into a mindless drone for them. The

Imperium would simply kill me.

I was screwed whatever happened.

I felt a wave pass through me and the black cubes started to slowly tap on the glass.

Shit. This was exactly what I didn't want. These cubes had to be testing how to get to me and then kill me.

I looked around the bridge and thankfully I had stolen two brand-new environmental suits from the last owners of this shuttle so I went over to the back of the bridge.

I slowly removed a large grey panel in the smooth walls and I smiled at the two bright red environmental suits. A loud high-pitched buzz echoed around me making me jump.

The black cubes were glowing red at me and I couldn't help but feel like the cubes were trying to warn me against putting on the suit.

To hell with them. They were going to kill me anyway so I might as well make the job a little bit harder for them.

I took out the two suits and each one had a small metal backpack on them with all the oxygen recyclers and air filters inside so I decided to disconnect one backpack on one suit and connect it to the other suit.

I had heard rumours of people using two backpacks before and it worked fine. Hell the suits were actually designed for three air-filtering backpacks but budget cuts made them reduce the number down to one.

The high-pitch scream got even louder and I stopped dead in my tracks.

I heard the deafening sound of glass cracking around me.

I couldn't waste any more time so I got the environmental suit on as quickly as possible and I activated the backpack.

Choking green gas filled my environment suit. I shut off the power but it was too late.

I ripped off my helmet and collapse to the ground as the choking green gas filtered out into the bridge and I felt my lungs burn in agony.

My vision blurred for a few moments and I seriously hated everything that was happening to me.

My eyes were so watery that I only heard the smashing of the windows but oddly enough no air rushed out and I wasn't sucked out into space.

I just sat there with my lungs burning up and I could have saw I felt icy cold liquid start to fill them. I had heard plenty of times about dry drowning and how toxic gas made the lungs drown themselves.

I just hadn't ever wanted it to happen to me.

I rolled over onto my back and rolled my eyes as I watched the three little cubes hover around me like bees inspecting a new plant to devour but the sound was unreal. Each of the cubes were singing a soothing melody and relaxed me, made me happy and made me very, very sleepy.

I fought to stay awake and the crippling pain filled my senses was overwhelming and I didn't want to fall asleep as my lungs filled with oxygen.

I coughed loudly enough to drown out the sweet melody of the cubes but they only got louder and within seconds my world collapsed around me.

***

"He should be waking up… now,"

My eyes snapped open and I gasped at the absolutely beautiful woman in front of me. The woman standing over me had long sexy blond hair, a radiant smile and a shockingly stunning face that was angles and lines.

She might have been wearing a long innocent white dress but that also made me perfectly aware that I was naked and I wasn't even on a bed.

I looked around at a very beautiful large white domed room I was in. It had to be some kind of hospital room but instead of the undertone of death, destruction and harsh cleaning chemicals I had known from watching my mother die in the Imperium. This hospital room smelt delightful of flowers.

The sound of people laughing, singing and talking about sports outside my room made me smile because this sure as hell wasn't the Imperium, so maybe I had died and gone to where dead people go after death.

The woman smiled at me and sadly stepped away from me so I was blinded by a bright beautiful sun and a large crystal clear blue sky that stretched on endlessly through a domed window. I wasn't on the first floor but I was amazed at the sheer scale of the breath-taking domed city I was in.

"Welcome to the Enlightened Republic Hayden," the woman said.

I had no idea how the woman knew my name but I was glad she did.

"I am Supreme General Abbie of the Enlightened Republic so I'm in charge of greeting the new arrivals from the Imperium," she said.

I just smiled. I had heard so many rumours of the Enlighted Republic and it just seemed impossible to believe that it was actually real and not some strange figure of humanity's imagination.

A republic that believed in hope, democracy and freedom. Three ideals that formed the great core of this Republic but I knew they were alien concepts to the Imperium.

"I have a lot to learn don't I?" I asked.

Abbie laughed beautifully and nodded. "Of course you do but so do so many others. We have thousands of drones all over the Imperium watching for anyone approaching us in case they want to kill us, but we also use them to know when someone needs help,"

I could only nod I was so glad that the cubes were friends, not foes.

"The sweet melody was designed by my daughter working on brain frequency and brain activity to help an injured person fall to sleep before we teleported them back here for treatment,"

"Thank you and, what happens to me now?" I asked.

Abbie gave me a very warm smile and she gestured I go over to the domed window so I did. The window was large but the view outside was simply stunning.

For as far as I could see there were people happy, singing and dancing in the wide open streets with a thriving market below selling all sorts of things. Of course some people were rushing to work and others were couples kissing in the street.

And that was a hell of a culture shock. People could never kiss in public, sell goods outside of Rex-approved channels and they certainly couldn't dance in the street.

"This is the future," Abbie said.

I could only smile as I realised that she was right. The Enlightened Republic was a hell of a future because I would finally be free and that really was the most precious thing of all and I was looking forward to exploring, helping and living in this wonderfully new world that had yet to be explored by me.

AUTHOR OF AGENTS OF THE EMPEROR SERIES

CONNOR WHITELEY

AMONGST THE ENEMY

A SCIENCE FICTION FAR FUTURE SHORT STORY

AMONGST THE ENEMY

This was the day I died.

I, Intelligence Officer Isaac Oldman, sat in the middle of an icy cold purple prison cell made from pure crystal. The prison cell wasn't too ugly, in fact it definitely had a certain beauty about it that I was shocked about.

I really enjoyed watching little creatures or whatever the foul alien Keres put into their magic crystals, as they pulsed, swirled and twirled around inside the stunning crystal. It was rather hypnotic in a strange way.

The prison cell itself wasn't much bigger than me but that was the strange thing about Keres technology, it very much had an evil mind of its own. If I wanted to stand up, the prison cell would get larger, if I wanted to sit down the entire cell would get a hell of a lot smaller. It was creepy that way and the sheer darkness of the purple crystal didn't allow me to see anything outside.

Thankfully I was an intelligence officer from the Imperial Secret Service so I was used to travelling beyond the holy realm of the Imperium and traveling into the darkness and coldness and foulness of the galaxy outside. It was only two years ago I was inside the so-called Enlightened Republic, the foul breakaway regions that were building nuclear weapons to destroy the Imperium once and for all.

All whilst they pretended to build a traitorous democracy. As if humans could actually rule themselves without the Rex's guiding light. It was just laughable.

But I knew how the foul Keres worked so I was probably stuck on some Rex-forsaken moon with thousands of other prisoners. Yet unlike me those other prisoners were probably not righteous, for only humanity would rule the stars and soon humanity would annihilate the Keres once and for all.

And then their evil magic could be erased from the universe.

Maybe I should have given the Keres more credit though, I was basically naked at this point with only a thin purple sheet around me. I had no doubt it was covered in magic and the foul aliens were searching my mind, thankfully my training had covered those stupid basics so the Keres were never going to get my secrets.

The air was sweet and filled with hints of grapes, grapefruit and blood oranges. Yet knowing exactly how evil these aliens were they were probably the smells of their own kind that they were sacrificing to their own gods and goddesses, the Keres were beasts at heart.

At least the sweet smells left the great taste of fruit salad on my tongue exactly how my mother used to make it.

The sweet aromas got even stronger and I hated myself for daring to confirm the thoughts of the weird magic of the Keres. They were probably wanting to lure me into their mind games using smells but I was a human, I was righteous, I wouldn't be tempted by their witchery.

In fact I was just glad that I was okay and I sent off all my information to the wonderful Imperial authorities before these beasts captured me.

At least now the Imperium had a fighting chance against the awful predations of the Keres.

Let me tell you exactly what I sent them.

***

+++Transmission Recording+++

Dear Lord Eraser,

Apologies for the lateness of my call but these beasts are far more intelligent than we ever gave them credit for, they know what humans are and they actively hunt them down. We need to exterminate them as soon as possible, and how the hell we didn't annihilate them after the Great War is beyond me.

I am not questioning His wisdom just the consequences of the action.

I am currently laying on top of an immense purple crystal rooftop on top of the Keres version of a holy skyscraper. I have to admit I am more than impressed with the sheer straightness, perfection and smoothness of the sides of the building.

I had no idea creatures could make such a building out of pure purple crystal. This seems to be the location of where the Keres live, they create vast purple cities filled with these skyscrapers to live in.

At some point I might seek to gain entrance into these abominable buildings but I must be patient my Lord. I know the Keres might be tracking my transmission so by the Rex I must be careful.

For as far as I can see the buildings rise up like immense purple daggers veiling the sky, ground and mountains like each hab-block (though I doubt that is what these monsters call their buildings) are like fortifications. I will seek to access their weakness so if an attack is needed we can bomb them in their sleep.

Which thankfully my Lord I can confirm the Keres do need. It is currently midnight on the planet and there is much less traffic about. The bright purple metal pods that the Keres use as transports are far fewer right now than they were earlier. You should have seen them my Lord, it was disgusting, huge purple streaks of pods through the sky.

It was an abomination to humanity's birthright and was nothing compared to the holy whiteness of our shuttles. It makes me sick just mentally sending this to you.

The air stinks, my lord, of foul oranges, grapefruits and grapes. This I must investigate further to make sure this is a food source and not some kind of biological weaponry, but I will confess the sheer silence of the city concerns me greatly.

There are no sounds of their awful high-pitched language, no shuttles zooming about the rest. This is most unnatural and I will admit my fear of exploring this most alien of worlds is building.

I will continue my mission for the Rex.

+++Transmission Send+++

***

+++Transmission Signal Searching+++
+++Transmission Signal Found and Sending+++

Immense bangs, pops and explosions echo around me my Lord as I enter a huge purple crystal "factory". That is what this place must be because it is so different to all the other types of buildings I have explored so far.

This building like all the others is simply made from living purple crystal with little strange lights that pulse, swirl and twirl around inside. I feel like they are looking at me half the time and I hate these creatures, I hate aliens and I can feel the cold fearful sweat drop down my back.

I am a warrior my Lord. I am not a recon specialist but I do not seek to question the Rex.

The "factory" was amazing as I watched the long lines of purple crystals, metals and corpses float up in the cold air in long, long lines high above me. If any of those corpses were still alive then I would probably look like some random ant or something.

The factory was so huge and I was so tiny.

Yet it was the silence that still infuriated me. I was used to so much sound, so much noise, so much joy but I couldn't hear anything.

So I did the only logical thing my Lord and I followed the endlessly long lines for as long as I could. I followed it to a large purple crystal balcony that overlooked a stunning pit of some sort.

I was amazed at it because the Keres were here. So many evil, corrupt, demonic Keres were here and I had a weapon on me, but I had to focus on the mission.

Recon only.

All the evil Keres were so thin with their tiny waists, largeish chests and sharp pointy humanoid features that it was simply disgusting, and a perversion of the Rex's divine Will. It was disgraceful that these aliens ever believed the Rex would allow them to look so close to humans.

I studied the females in their long black dresses that swept across the floor with long blond pieces of hair floating up like the air and constantly moving, almost like they were scanning the air.

I just hoped these creatures weren't intelligent enough to detect me.

The Keres stood in their long lines and as soon as a shard of crystal, a chunk of metal and a chunk of a corpse floated past, they would simply click their fingers and in a bright flash of magical light they would become weapons.

I saw guns, rocket launchers and laser swords being created.

And by the Rex did this annoy me. These Keres actually dared to create arms, armour and evil weapons against the righteousness of humanity that was disgusting and I wanted nothing more than to simply slaughter them all.

This was in direct violation of the Treaty of Defeat that these pathetic creatures signed after they lost the war.

Then everything stopped.

All the Keres looked directly at me.

They thrusted out their hands.

Magical fireballs zoomed towards me.

I ran like hell.

The enemy knew I was here.

+++Transmission sent+++

***

+++Transmission Sending+++

Dear Lord Eraser,

I need an urgent evacuation and urgent military reinforcements sent to my location immediately. The problem is far, far worse than I ever could have imagined.

The Keres were more demonic than we ever thought possible.

After the Keres started to hunt me down, I managed to escape into some kind of sewage network and it was mightily impressive because all the waste created by this society is simply magically teleported down into the sewer tunnels and they end up into a conversion chamber.

Then magic turns the waste into something useful again.

Of course I had to kill three foul Keres males to get you that information but it was worth it, and the entire Keres race will hopefully burn for it.

Anyway my Lord, after I escaped I knew the Keres were going to use their abominable magic to hunt me down so I decided to invade their homes, learn some more information and hopefully learn a secret to their undoing.

Let me tell you my Lord, our reports and beliefs and information about the Keres living like plebs couldn't be further from the truth.

I'm currently leaning against a bright purple wall made of pure crystal in some of the apartments and every single apartment is open concept, open plan and open everything. I do not believe these creatures even know what a door is.

Instead of sofas, they had a strange orange floating thing in front of a row of pink diamonds, which I now believe is a type of communication network using their magic to power it all.

I tried to get the young Keres woman to show how it worked but she refused, so I killed her.

The kitchen area is even stranger my Lord, because there are no holo-freezers, holo-ovens or even a food synthesiser. There are just bowls of huge blue melons and I think the Keres just magic up their food and drink.

That is what another young man was doing before I stormed in and killed him.

It is no wonder these aliens are so dumb and inferior to humanity. Maybe these lazy aliens learnt how to cook instead of filling their bodies with magic then maybe their species wouldn't be as braindead as humanity.

Thankfully that just makes killing them easier.

But my biggest concern is the massive bright orange, glowing sack on the bright white ceiling. It concerns me because I believe there were small, baby Keres inside.

Every so often when the bright orange sack flashes, I can see small fingers, small legs and small faces just staring me at smiling, laughing and waiting for something bad to happen.

Of course I would never kill these baby Keres because that is not what the Rex wants. He requires baby Keres to be indoctrinated into the ways of humanity so they see their own species as corrupt and evil, and in the end the Keres will annihilate themselves and become slaves for humanity.

That is why the Rex is so clever because he is always so much further ahead of the enemy.

But this concerns me greatly because all these apartments that I have broken into have these orange sacks above them. I don't like this and this means that instead of the Keres population dying off like we believed.

It was actually growing and that means the Keres will soon be able to raise an army against us.

We must be ready.

Someone's coming.

+++Transmission sent+++

***

I have to admit I didn't expect the Keres to simply click their fingers and knock me out when one of their military commanders in their golden, ornate armour stormed and took me prisoner.

I just stared at the bright white lights flashing about in my purple prison cell as I realised that I shouldn't have been able to remember those things. I was an intelligence officer and my mind was a fortress and once I did something in the Rex's name I shouldn't have been able to remember it, much less recall it inside an enemy prison.

A sweet musical laughter echoed all around me as the purple drained away from the crystal to become see-through. I just frowned as I saw I was isolated in the middle of nowhere on some damn moon.

For as far as I could see there was only endless amounts of grey rock, there were no people, no signs of life and no other signs of prisoners. There was just me alone and I knew I was about to die.

I had read a lot of intelligence reports over the years and I knew how the immoral Keres worked. As soon as the crystal prison cell went away I would choke to death and I wouldn't be able to scream.

There would be no air at all.

The sweet aromas of blood oranges, grapefruit and grapes went away to be replaced with the cold smell of dust. Because in the end that was all what the galaxy was, one single massive sheet of dust, rock and death.

"Thank you for revealing your mind to me," a human woman said into my mind.

"I did not reveal anything to you, and why do you work for the Keres? If this is mental conditioning then fight back, fight for humanity, fight for the Rex," I said with authority.

The woman laughed inside my mind. "You are a fool little man because the Keres are innocent creatures that humanity were scared of. We slaughtered their race for nothing except fear and now I am making things right by helping them,"

"Traitor. Murderer. Evil woman,"

"Call me whatever you want but I know the truth Isaac and I know what is coming for humanity and the Keres. A force so great that only the Goddess Genitrix can save us,"

I just laughed at the stupidity of this woman, clearly she had fallen for the delusional ideology and mythology of the Keres. The idea that the Big Bang was caused by the birth of a Goddess of Life and a God of Death and the Keres were created to guard life and humanity was born to destroy all life and serve the God of Death.

It was stupid and I honestly pitted this pathetic woman.

"You can never change so I will release you from your fleshy body and I just pray to Genetrix that she grabs your soul before He does,"

I was about to protest out loud when I noticed the crystal prison cell was gone and I could no longer breathe.

"And thank you for the transmissions," the woman said. "They never reached the Imperium and I will always fight against your corrupt oppressive empire,"

My eyes just widened in horror as I collapsed gasping for air that wasn't there and I just hoped that the Keres would all die out because they were evil, I had seen that first-hand and I bore witness to their foulness because I had lived amongst the enemy.

And now I could happily die for my sins.

AUTHOR OF AGENTS OF THE EMPEROR SERIES
CONNOR WHITELEY

CORRUPTING DARKNESS
A SCIENCE FICTION FAR FUTURE SHORT STORY

CORRUPTING DARKNESS

Thick choking aromas of smoke, charred flesh and boiling blood filled Captain Henry Oblong's senses as his eyes slowly flickered open. He had no idea where he was, how he had gotten here or what was actually happening.

All he could do was focus on the terrible, ugly, awful smell that seemed to fill the air like the evil cousin of oxygen was trying to replace it. Henry coughed and he just wanted to be okay. He hated the foul taste of charred flesh that formed on his tongue.

Henry didn't want to be on some strange alien world. He wanted to be protecting humanity, saving people's lives and just helping to make sure humanity lasted one day at a time in this cold deadly galaxy.

He slowly tried to move his hands side to side to feel what he was on or at least touching, he was surprised by the sheer icy coldness of the sandy ground beneath him. He realised he was on his back, winded and he was struggling to breathe.

Henry really tried to remember why the hell he was here. He was an Imperial soldier he knew that, he had enlisted when he was 16 to make sure that humanity was protected against the traitors, aliens and the so-called magic that certain alien races were corrupted by.

Henry had no idea at all why he was on his back on a planet filled with such an awful atmosphere. It was so disgusting that he actually wanted to be sick but real soldiers do not vomit. That was the golden rule of the Imperium.

After a few more seconds of choking and struggling to breathe, Henry forced himself up and he really focused on his surroundings.

He was surprised that there was nothing around him except the burning, crackling and popping wreckage of bright a white pod that he had been travelling in. Henry was meant to meet up with a massive Imperial fleet that was gathering in the area to scourge the aliens off these worlds.

As much as Henry wanted to go over to the pod, he sadly knew there was nothing he could do now. The pod was destroyed and Henry guessed it was hardly natural for an Imperial pod to get blown out the sky. It was probably shot, bombed or maybe some foul magic had forced it to land.

Henry hated aliens and he was going to kill them all in the end.

Henry forced his attention away from the pod and hated the sheer thickness of the black smoke that swirled, twirled and whirled around him. It didn't seem natural because there wasn't any wind, there were no forces at play here to explain what he was seeing and Henry didn't like how he felt like he was being watched.

The coldness of the air made him shiver and Henry realised that unless he made it to shelter or something soon. He was going to die and then humanity had one less soldier to defend itself with. Something he absolutely couldn't allow.

Henry forced himself to take a step forward then another then another.

Henry felt like he was swimming through pea soup or something just as harsh, cold and evil. He had thankfully heard and studied and killed more magical aliens, Keres, than he cared to think about but this wasn't their style.

The Keres were a dying out alien race that were weak, pathetic and evil down to their very core. Yet their pathetic-ness made them cowards at heart so they were all about ambushing and this wasn't ambushing.

Henry could have sworn he saw shadows and figures move in the darkness of the smoke but as soon as he blinked they were gone.

The smoke burnt his eyes and caused water to stream down his face this was a nightmare and he hated every single minute of it.

He felt around for his gun, knife and pistol that he always carried on his waist but they were gone. Henry swore under his breath as he forced himself to continue.

If the enemy had shot him down then there was no telling what he was dealing with so the only ally he had here was higher ground so he could hopefully get out of this damn smoke.

Then he took a step that changed everything.

Henry stepped forward and jerked himself as he no longer felt sand under his feet but something hard and shiny and awful as he found himself in a brand-new black crystal chamber.

He had no clue what had just happened but this was bad. The chamber was large made from shiny black crystal that pulsed with blood red energy and Henry felt like he was meant to touch it.

He knew that would be a bad idea if there ever was one.

The air stunk of charred flesh, ash and death as Henry paced around hoping for a way out of the chamber but there wasn't one.

The domed ceiling made from shiny black crystal was even brighter with blood red energy than the sides, and Henry really wanted to escape.

The crystal walls of the prison hummed, vibrated and banged. Henry broke into a fighting stance and then he swore the foul aliens that he had never thought he would see behind this most unholy act against humanity.

Out of the crystal walls a single very tall and scarily thin humanoid female stepped out. Blood red energy glowed on her pale white skin and face and body where veins and arties should have been.

Henry just focused on the female's pointy, sharp face that he was fairly sure could be used as a weapon in its own right. She was a Keres but definitely not one of the aliens he had seen before.

The female swirled her hand and red magical energy made the air crackle as she smiled.

"Captain Henry," the female said, her human tongue harsh, unrefined and just plain awful.

Henry wanted to kill her there and then. All the foul Keres knew that under the Treaty of Defeat attacking humanity was the worst possible crime, punishable by extermination.

Of course humanity was allowed to kill the Keres as they pleased but if the Keres were less bestial then they might have won the war instead of being defeated like the pathetic creatures they were.

"I was excited to meet such a kill like yourself," the female said her voice becoming more and more of an echo. "I had wondered by the glory of Geneitor would make our paths cross,"

Henry just rolled his eyes. It was beyond pathetic of the Keres to believe in their flawed and unholy mythology about how a God called Geneitor had created death and sought to kill all life but the Mother of Creation Genetrix sought to protect it.

"Release me demon," Henry said. "Your race is breaking the law and I will burn you for it,"

The female smiled. "Then my species does not have much of an incentive to do that, does it? And I have much more important uses for you in the services of Geneitor,"

"I will never turn, I will never reveal secrets and I will always protect humanity,"

The female laughed. "Every single human says that when I capture them but they always turn,"

"I am not a normal human," Henry said. "I am a soldier, a hero of humanity and I am a killer of the Keres,"

The female shivered in pleasure and Henry wanted to be sick.

"His Lordship is grateful for the souls of the murdered so thank you. They keep him powerful, stirring and strong enough to one day return to this dying galaxy so he can complete what the foul Mother stopped him from doing," she said.

Henry shook his head.

He charged.

The female clicked her fingers and Henry froze. He tried to

fight, scream, kick. He couldn't do anything.

"Humans are always so inelegant and you haven't asked me who I am," the female said. "My name is The Corrupter, a champion of Geneitor and it is my job to corrupt the souls of Keres and humans alike so they may serve him even in death,"

Henry laughed. He had never heard of such rubbish in all his life.

"Let us take a little trip around my encampment,"

Before Henry could ever think about protesting, choking blood red smoke engulfed him and he felt the world fall away from him.

***

Henry was hardly impressed with the stupid Corrupter as he found himself alone standing in the middle of a massive group of skin-crafted tents with a roaring, crackling fire in the middle.

He had to admit that tents were domed, ugly and Henry realised he didn't need to have magic to know that they were crafted out of human skin, there was even some blood and muscle still attached to some sheets of skin flapping about in the coldness of the air.

He enjoyed the scents of flowers, jasmine and chilli in the air before it was leaving replaced with the foul scent of charred flesh that was so strong in the air he was almost choking. He hated the Keres.

The flames of the fire danced a little and a moment later the Corrupter appeared smiling at him in fiery form.

"It is amazing that you believe we are Keres, but we are Dark Keres, Fallen Keres or Shadow Walkers depending on what idiots you ask about us," the Corrupter said.

"Why bring me here? Why not just kill me and let your false God feast on my soul?" Henry asked knowing that Geneitor was nothing more than a myth created by a dying alien race.

The Corrupter laughed. "Look around you Captain Henry,"

Henry nodded as he stared at the skin-crafted tents and how cold, unloved and isolated each of them looked. Then he saw long feral claws were reaching out of the tents.

"This is what I have had to do to save Keres race. Souls keep

Geneitor alive long enough for his influence to spread but the Great War must be fought and the Keres race must be saved,"

"What are you talking about? Your race is an abomination that deserves to die," Henry said.

Henry walked round to the other side of the fire and he was surprised that not a single hint of warmth came from it.

"When humanity attacked my home planet, burnt my village, killed my entire family. I escaped into the Ultraspace network, you know that intergalactic transport system you stole from us,"

Henry smiled. That was definitely one of the greatest benefits of the war and it was so worth all the bloodshed that righteous humanity had committed.

"I was about to die in the network when Geneitor found me, he convinced me to serve him and he shared some of his power with me. He gave me the secret to destroying humanity and saving the Keres race,"

Henry shook his head. These aliens deserved to die and there was nothing she could say that would convince him otherwise.

"I need to find the Stones of Geneitor and bring him into this universe so we can wipe out humanity once and for all. Then my race can be safe again with the God of Death looking over us,"

Henry spat at her. "If your God is so powerful then why can my species kill you all so easily,"

"The Dark Keres are outcasts, hunted by the mainstream Keres in case humanity learn about us and wage war against us once more. The Keres are scared and look at what the Dark Keres have been reduced to,"

Henry didn't care that these aliens had been reduced to living out of skin-crafted tents, forced to eat corpse meat off the bone judging by the bones littering the campsite, and he really didn't care the Dark Keres were weak.

"You are a dying race and that is it," Henry said. "You cannot make anything, you cannot protect yourself, you cannot do anything,"

The Corrupter sighed. "That is all true and we have no need for money or trade because the gifts of the Destroyer but I was hoping to turn you more easily but watch what I show you next. This is the truth,"

Henry was about to protest when his mind started to fill with images of dying humans, men and women just being murdered by other humans. There were images of corruption and evil bargains being struck in the highest levels of Imperial Government and more images revealed the creation of super weapons.

Henry knew they were being created to be used against the Enlightened Republic, the stupid breakaway regions of humanity that believed in democracy against the righteous control of the Rex.

So many innocent humans would be destroyed simply because they chose democracy over the Rex. That was wrong and Henry didn't want that.

The people of the Enlightened Republic needed to be sent to re-education camps not killed.

"Geneitor could save them all," The Corrupter said. "You once mentioned to a friend that your purpose is to save humanity, protect it and keep innocent people alive,"

Henry nodded that was the entire point of his being.

"If you join Geneitor I can promise you that these people will be saved, protected and live alongside the Keres. The Republic has no problem with my race so they will not be killed,"

Henry had to agree with her there. He knew the Imperium would wipe out all non-Imperial fractions sooner or later that meant a lot of innocent people dying.

Henry looked at the Corrupter. "Are there such things as innocent Keres?"

The Corrupter stepped out of fire returning to her flesh and blood form. Her pale white face smiling at him.

"Me and Geneitor can promise you that the Keres did not start this war. Humanity was scared of our power and that made them shoot first,"

Henry felt something start to press against his mind. It felt so pleasurable, calming and safe like it was a parent offering him a hug, maybe the Keres were not so bad after all and if humanity was capable of so much murder and bloodshed then maybe they did need to be stopped with Genitor's help.

That way he could continue to help humanity, save lives and just protect every single human he had always wanted to do ever since he was 16 years old.

"What will happen to me when I convert?" Henry asked.

The Corrupter smiled and hugged him. "Nothing bad. You will simply accept Geneitor into your heart, mind and body. You will become stronger, tougher and see the universe in a brand-new way,"

Henry nodded. It sounded scary as hell but he had to protect humanity no matter the cost.

"But I will warn you if you choose this path then humanity will hunt you down, mainstream Keres will hunt you down and so will the Daughters of Generatrix. Is that a risk you would want to take?"

Henry nodded.

The Corrupter smiled and Henry's mind exploded as he became a Dark Keres.

***

Six months later, Henry smiled as he stood on a massive desert planet covered in golden sand for as far as the eye could see. There were no dunes, no hills nor mountains but Henry was more than glad about that. It meant there were basically no places for the evil humans to run away to.

The air stunk of jasmine, flowers and mint that left the great taste of mint ice cream form on his tongue. He had no idea why the humans had choked and coughed and hissed in pain as they breathed in the air but that was the stupid thing about humans they just didn't know what was good for them.

Henry gripped his bone spear tightly as his fellow Keres came over to him. They all looked so great, angelic and beautiful with their long claws, bone spikes shooting out of their armour and their long fangs looked perfect as they dripped small amounts of blood onto the ground.

Henry still couldn't believe it had taken so long for him to accept Genitor's gifts because that was the thing about the Destroyer, he was never a bad man, he didn't destroy people's minds. He only gave them the tools to realise that the galaxy was an evil place and humanity was the greatest challenge they faced.

Humanity had to die to make sure the Keres survived and that was all that mattered.

Henry licked his fangs with his hard snake tongue as he looked forward to hunting down the rest of the humans on the planet and sacrifice their fat juicy souls to Genitor and hopefully some of them would even see the enlightenment that the Destroyer had offered him.

Humanity was going to pay for their sin of existence and Henry had no problem with that at all.

It was going to be a beautifully dark and bloody future, exactly what the God of Death wanted and Henry didn't want to disappoint his Lord and Master. Not for a single second.

AUTHOR OF AGENTS OF THE EMPEROR SERIES

CONNOR WHITELEY

ASHES OF VALICAN
A SCIENCE FICTION FAR FUTURE SHORT STORY

ASHES OF VALICAN

An entire world was burnt to ash in a matter of minutes.

When I, Elizabeth Sobeth, was summoned to investigate the events of Valican, I hardly doubted it was anything more than a simple case of a planet being miscategorised by the idiots of the Imperium and their so-called divine Rex.

What I actually found terrified me.

According to scans, maps and a number of highly rated travel books, I should have been standing in the middle of a luscious ocean with amazing colourful fish, monsters and tourists would come here for months at a time to sail on these stunning seas.

Believe me that couldn't be further from the truth because I was standing in the middle of an ash-covered stretch of land that really did go on endlessly for miles upon miles. There was nothing here for ash that was constantly getting blown up and kicked into the air by a harsh warm breeze.

The ash was an interesting mixture of black, grey and yellow that constantly swirled around each other in weird alien ways that I didn't understand.

I wanted to believe it was nothing more than damage from a massive fire but considering that there were no signs of life, no signs of water and no signs of anything on the planet, I knew I was just hoping for the impossible. Something or a group of people had killed an entire planet.

Thankfully, after I made my full report to Earth and the Rex himself, this would all be out of my hands. Because the very last thing that I wanted to do was deal with a group of aliens or humans that had the power to burn an entire world.

The sheer smell of ash, smoke and charred flesh filled my senses and clawed at my lungs. I wished I had bought my damn rebreather but that was impossible because I had left it on my black ship in orbit.

Something that I really didn't like about the planet besides the smell and walking on ash, was the sheer silence of the planet.

I had read the reports and documents in Imperial Records and this entire planet had hosted over two billion humans, it was a fairly advanced colony and the people were making a killing off the tourism trade.

So who could have done the annihilation of an entire planet so easily? There wasn't a call for help, any survivors or any sign that anyone knew what was happening.

I went off into the distance, hating how soft and crumbly the ash-covered ground felt under my feet and my stomach twisted in a painful knot at the idea of the ash collapsing and me falling into a pit.

That was a very real fear.

The sky was remarkably clear considering the sheer amount of ash on the ground. The sun was shining brightly off the intensely light ash so I was more than happy I was wearing a holo-visor, protecting my eyes from the intense UV light, and my robes were long so I shouldn't burn.

Yet I feared that burning and going blind were the least of my problems.

I kept walking through the ash covered wastelands, just hoping that I would find something to tell me what had happened.

I always carried a small black box device that allowed me to take air and ash samples but I had done that earlier. The air was perfectly okay and the oxygen levels seemed to be increasing oddly enough despite the lack of trees on Valican.

"Do you know me?" a voice said behind me.

I stopped instantly because no one was there a minute ago so I turned around and jumped.

A woman was sitting there.

I just focused on the tall, very thin woman just sitting there like she was dying or something. I knew she was from the planet because she was wearing the traditional long white robes of this culture and golden rings were wrapped around her neck. One for each of the so-called Great Beasts she had killed.

Apparently on Valican there were ten Beasts that a person needed to kill to be ruler of the planet. The Rex had always found that detail funny so he allowed the humans to continue that weird tradition even under his tyrannical rule.

And yes I do realise everything I have already said in this report is more than enough to get me executed for treason against the Rex. But oh well.

The woman had nine of the rings around her neck and her face was smiling but her lips were cracked and her eyes were glassy. She was blind and she was looking right at me.

And I could have sworn she was staring into my soul.

"I don't know you," I said. "I am Doctor Elizabeth of the Imperial Science Division,"

"Are you here about the monsters and the Space Children?" the woman asked.

I hated how I had to remember every single little detail about this weird culture. She knew that the Rex normally burnt worlds for believing in any being besides him but this world had humoured him for some reason.

I wish my own home planet was that lucky.

"What are the Star Children?" I asked.

"The creatures you call the Keres that came down from the skies in screaming pods of purple, black and blue. They howled and roared and screamed bloody murder in the name of their dark God Geneitor," the woman said.

Valican grabbed her stomach. She felt it knot and churn

violently. She had faced the Dark Keres before, magical alien beings that wanted to resurrect their God of Death so he could wipe out humanity and save the Keres race from annihilation.

Annihilation that humanity had unjustly started. Again that simple sentence would so get me murdered by the Rex.

"What happened here?" I asked kneeling down on the ash-covered ground so I was at least eye-level with the woman. She followed my gaze perfectly.

It was so creepy.

"We were all just minding our own business. I was feeding young girls in the market and listening to them talking about dates they were going on later tonight. That is when the sun went out for a minute as the pods of the Dark Keres screamed out,"

I jerked backwards slightly because this woman wasn't what she was pretending to be, because not a single human outside of the highest levels of Imperial government and rarely the Imperial Army knew there was a difference between the Dark Keres, Keres and the Daughters of Generatrix. Another offshoot of the Keres race that wanted to resurrect their Goddess of Life to safeguard the Keres race.

"Who are you?" I asked.

The woman grinned. "A trickster some say. A monster others say. What do you call me Doctor Sobeth?"

She knew who I was. That couldn't be possible and that was just wrong on so many levels.

"You want to tell me what you and your people did to this world," I said knowing this foul alien probably wanted to kill me as much as I wanted to kill it.

"We needed souls for Geneitor. He was hungry and our warband was interested in burning a world for the fun of it and we wanted to unleash the Incarnation,"

I shivered at the very mention of the Incarnation. I had heard it mentioned a lot of times in hushed voices when I was serving alongside a detachment of Imperial special forces.

No one had ever seen the creatures but the rumours were powerful enough. It was said that once there were enough murders, spilled blood and screams on a battlefield that The Champion of Death could summon a shard of Geneitor's soul into the galaxy.

In the form of a demonic monster known as the Incarnation. A creature so powerful, monstrous and deadly that entire armies could explode in minutes.

"Did you summon him?" I asked really knowing I had to find a way to kill this woman before she killed me.

"No," the woman said sounding disappointed. "That was not what caused the death of your world. The death of your world was more sudden than a simple battle and I know the Dark Keres were not behind it,"

I shook my head. She had to be lying. The Dark Keres had attacked this innocent human world so the killers had to be them. Right?

"You are a clever soul Doctor. You know I can sense Geneitor wanted to lick and taste your soul so you will be killed at some point. I know that would make my Master happy but you must look closer to home to find out who had murdered your people,"

She charged.

Jumping on me.

She punched me.

Fangs shot out of her.

I gripped her fangs.

They glowed blood red.

Burning my hands.

I snapped them.

Thrusting them into the woman's head.

The woman laughed loudly as I killed her and I kept stabbing her until she didn't laugh anymore.

But if what she said was true then I needed to return to my ship and research if the Imperium had ordered this murder.

And if the Dark Keres had simply come here to feast on the

souls because they knew the humans were already going to die.

***

As much as I didn't like my small, cramped research ship that was nothing more than a black circular sphere with only one room in the entire ship, I had to admit that it did have excellent research capabilities.

I sat in a giant black metal chair holding a small holo-reader as I scanned Imperial archives of what had happened to Valican over its lifetime and what top-secret projects were rumoured to live here.

The rest of the ship was only the size of a swimming pool but it was filled with so many holo-readers, pieces of research equipment and food containers because I wasn't allowed a food synthesiser there was barely any room left for me.

I hated the ship almost as much as I hated the Rex himself.

Anyway, the archives showed that Valican was once a death world because it was so far away from the sun that it couldn't possibly support any forms of life. Yet these are exactly the sort of worlds that the Dark Keres love to hide on.

When Valican was first encountered by Imperial forces, they found two warbands of Dark Keres on the surface, so they were murdered and the planet suddenly became filled with trees, animals and oceans.

At the time no one cared because this was right after the Treaty of Defeat was signed so the Keres race had lost the war, humanity was basically subtly enslaving them and the human race was safe whilst they continued to murder a peaceful species.

But I now believe this was a trick done by the being known as Geneitor to lure humans to the world so he could kill them at a later date.

I had to sadly readjust myself in my metal chair because the icy coldness of space was seeping more and more into my ship. That meant the damn heater and engine systems were failing.

I didn't have long left to discover the truth before I had to flee and stop my search.

However, as much as I like that theory I have to admit it is wrong. Since the problem with Imperial Records on Geneitor is even though I have heard rumours of the Rex acknowledging the existence of the Keres God and Goddess he refuses to allow research on them so the majority of humanity did not fall to their corrupting influence.

I sort of understand that.

Anyway, the small amount of data I can find about Geneitor is that he never ever creates life. He only kills it so the idea he could create an entire planet filled with trees just to lure in humans seemed impossible.

So I believe humanity used a terraforming technology that was not documented and that led to the creation of Valican.

A much more likely theory has to come from the Lord Planetary Governor of Valican himself because before he was assassinated and the Rex himself directly ruled over the planet, he confessed to a series of nuclear experiments.

Since the Planetary Governor wanted to learn why and how humanity had almost annihilated Earth before using this technology. And as much as the Rex's supporters claimed the ruler of humanity cleared out the planet of nuclear waste, I know the Rex would never do that.

A weapon is a weapon and nuclear weapons would be like the best present ever to the Rex.

There's no way in hell he destroyed them so there is a good chance these nuclear weapons went off during the attack of the Dark Keres.

I readjusted myself in my chair yet again as I shivered and I noticed my breath started to form long columns of vapour. I was running out of time before I had to make a jump to somewhere safe.

I flicked over the page on my holo-reader and I realised what had actually happened to this planet and I realised just how evil the Imperium was.

Back in the Keres-Human War, I had helped and studied and built the supernova Destroyer Class warships that had a weapon so powerful that a single blast could destroy an entire planet in a second.

Of course that warship was thankfully annihilated by the Keres towards the end of the war but the technology always remained. In fact, I had seen the technology used in everything from guns to missiles to laser weapons.

And an old boyfriend had told me that the supernova technology had recently been changed to superheat a planet and the Imperium was looking for testing sites.

Of course he wanted to know what planets I wanted dead, I said none, so I later found out that the Imperium had killed my ex-boyfriend for failing to find a planet. The Imperium was extremely weird like that.

A superheated blast would be more than possible to burn an entire world and if the Keres legends about Geneitor and Generatrix being able to sense life and death were true, then I have little doubt the God would have sent a warband there to make sure they collected the souls on his behalf.

I shivered at the very notion of what I had discovered and a small red flashing light appeared on my holo-console. I knew it was an Imperial Navy warship coming to kill me because that's the thing about the stupid Imperium.

You cannot say something against them. you cannot challenge them. And by the Rex, you certainly cannot discover the sheer power they hold because that means you know something they don't want you to know.

Meaning they cannot control you enough.

So I spun around on my black metal chair and with shaking hands I simply typed in coordinates to the Enlightened Republic, the little breakaway region of humanity that believed in peace, democracy and working with the Keres against the predations of the Imperium.

When I entered the Ultraspace network, a warning light told me three missiles were heading my way.

I zoomed off into the network and I was really looking forward to starting a brand-new life in the Republic, learning more about the

Dark Keres and helping to protect humanity from both itself and the dark powers that stirred in the divine.

Lines were being drawn and sooner or later a massive fight between humanity, the different divisions of the Keres and the Republic would happen. And I just hoped for the sake of the innocent, that the right side won.

The ashes of Valican would always remind me why fighting against the Imperium and the Dark Keres were the most important things imaginable.

ENFORCEMENT

This was the day he died and doomed all life in the galaxy forever.

Imperial Ambassador and Enforcer Adrian Shaw took an ugly purple crystal seat at the even darker purple crystal table where he was meant to be meeting one of the damn Keres aliens that humanity had the disservice of ruling over.

He smiled to himself as he sat in the large meeting room if he could actually call it that. Adrian really didn't like how the Keres made everything out of dark purple crystal that flashed, pulsed and hummed ever so slightly. It was a stupid way to design something and it was why he was more than glad humanity ruled over these criminal aliens.

Adrian had fought in the Human-Keres war multiple times, he had even been a General when the Treaty of Defeat was signed and now Adrian was really pleased he got to make sure the evil aliens were following the Treaty to the letter. This was just another calm meeting but Adrian could have sworn that everything just felt a little off.

In case he wasn't just imagining things, like his ex-wife claimed he did every single day, he focused on the perfectly smooth purple crystal walls next to him on both sides and behind him. The walls hardly seemed out of place, they were perfectly smooth, reflective and shiny like they always were.

Adrian couldn't deny that the Keres were evil enough to use

their foul, unnatural magic to try and manipulate him. But he was a human, a God in a galaxy filled with lesser creatures and it was his birthright to rule the stars.

He was simply too smart for the Keres to manipulate him.

Adrian ran his fingers over the perfectly, wonderfully warm crystal table. He really liked how the Keres were clever enough to use their foul magic to make sure everything was body temperature so nothing seemed hot nor cold and everything was good. He was surprised that the Keres were actually intelligent enough to do that.

The sweet aromas of vanilla, strawberries and mint made Adrian smile as the taste of strawberry shortcake formed on his tongue. His mother used to make the most amazing ones, and then Adrian realised he seriously needed to focus in case the foul magic was picking up on his surface thoughts to manipulate him.

It was stupid of the Keres to actually try something that evil so he stood up and went away from the awful chair and crystal and went towards the breathtaking view of the city below.

Adrian had lived in the Keres city for the past five years and it was okay for a stupid alien race. He almost respected the immense purple crystal shards that rose out of the ground and high into the purple sky. Those purple shards were meant to be buildings but Adrian had never wanted to go in one, it simply wasn't natural for something as divine as a human to go into as awful as a Keres building of all things.

He hated these aliens.

Adrian watched the little purple, blue and red crystal discs and pods float through the air as the lazy Keres transported themselves from place to place. He didn't mind them wanting to travel but it was stupid that these mere creatures didn't want to walk.

Having access to good transportation was surely only something creatures as divine as humanity was allowed to have. Adrian really wanted off this awful planet but the Treaty of Defeat had to be maintained no matter the cost and Adrian would do anything to make sure that happened.

Even if it meant annihilating this awful race once and for all.

"Enforcer," a female said behind him.

Adrian took in a deep breath of the vanilla, strawberry and mint scented air and he forced himself to turn around and look at the disgraceful form of the female Keres. The woman was sort of beautiful with her long, thin humanoid features with an unnaturally thin waist, long pretty neck and pointy elf-like features.

He didn't like looking at the awful Keres because it was like they were actually trying to make a mockery of the divinity of humanity. This woman was just as disgraceful as all the other versions of her kin.

"It is an honour to see you again," the woman said. "I can assure the Imperium and the Glorious Rex himself that Keres are living in ways conducive to the Treaty of Defeat,"

Adrian shook his head and took out a data slate. "That is a lie and you know it, Keres scum. The Treaty of Defeat Section 5c and 9a make it illegal for the Keres to have a form of social activity,"

"We do not have social activities," the woman said like Adrian was an idiot.

"Humans are the only people that are allowed social activity and they are gambling, smoking and clubbing," Adrian said. "The Keres are not allowed,"

"And I have yet to see any evidence of this so-called activities," the woman said and Adrian realised that she was now floating up in the air.

"Our spies took these photos of the Keres doing some kind of singing, dancing and partying," Adrian said passing the woman the photos.

Adrian hated to look at them because they were clearly dangerous, evil and beyond contempt to the righteousness of humanity. All the Keres in the photos were singing and dancing around some kind of corpse and it was just disgusting to look at.

The woman clicked her fingers and the air crackled. Adrian really wished he had bought a gun with him and a massive one at that.

"This isn't an example of social activity. These were taken two weeks ago I presume during the Feast of Life,"

Adrian rolled his eyes. He had no idea why humanity didn't just nuke this pointless alien race in the first place, especially with them continuing to bang on about their damn mythology.

He was aware of how the so-called Feast of Life was meant to honour the even more so-called Goddess of Life Genetrix. The woman that had apparently created humanity and Keres from different arms of hers.

"It is just stupid you continue to believe in lies," Adrian said hating this woman, "if you would simply abandon those ways then the Rex might treat you better,"

The woman grinned at him. "Enforcer, the problem with humanity is that you continue to ignore basic facts about the galaxy. In fact it is amazing you humans even manage to grasp the grandeur of the universe,"

Adrian really wished he had a gun about now. How dare this woman challenge the righteousness of humanity.

"All of us know that Genetrix and the God of Death Geneitor are alive and well. And their total rebirth can only happen when someone collects the Soul Stones of their God Children,"

Adrian laughed. Now she was being beyond stupid. The entire idea of Gods, Goddesses and their so-called divine children was just an insult.

As much as Adrian wanted to condemn this race for lunacy he sadly had other business to question.

"And there have been ten attacks on Imperial warships by Keres elements in the past year. That is a clear violation of the Treaty,"

"Yet humanity continues to massacre my people," the Keres woman said. "Tell me enforcer how many millions of my people have been murdered by humans in the past year,"

Adrian stood up and paced around the disgusting office for a moment. He didn't doubt that she was well aware of the disgraceful attacks against innocent humans and if this was part of a massive

Keres revenge plot then he had to find out what was happening.

He even considered he might have to be nice to her, a Keres of all things, to make sure she gave him the information.

"I don't know but I don't support murder of any kind," Adrian said as he felt a pressure building against his mind.

"You lie," the woman said. "You seek information human. I can see your thoughts as clear as day and you want to wipe out my race,"

Adrian fell to his knees as the pressure built and built.

"I can see your fear human," the woman said. "You might deny the existence of Genetrix but she gives me power and she sees your soul. You have murdered thousands in the name of your false divinity and now… you have attracted the sight of Geneitor,"

Adrian forced himself up despite the agony that was pouring out of his knees.

"That makes sense. Geneitor would want to corrupt young, stupid minds like humanity to serve him and actually I can show you the true grandeur of the galaxy if you want me to,"

Adrian instantly realised that this was no one from the normal Keres. This woman or whatever foul creature she had to be from one of the extremist factions that wanted to save the stupid Keres races.

Adrian reached for a gun that wasn't there and the woman laughed.

"Now meet your true God or learn the truth about the Keres. Tell us see what Fate Geneitor has chosen for you,"

Adrian screamed as he felt the world fall away from him.

***

He had no idea how long he was out for but Adrian was guessing maybe an hour or two. He found himself standing in the middle of some strange black sandy desert with a pitch black sky that he didn't recognise. He knew this couldn't be something in the known galaxy because it just didn't feel like it.

The entire area was icy cold and the awful wind that rushed past him reminded Adrian of being in a wind tunnel back at university, but the weird thing was that his hair wasn't moving. He could hear and see the wind. He couldn't feel it.

He tried to strain his eyes in an effort to see if anything was out here. Maybe there was a structure, maybe a fellow human or maybe there was something else anything.

It was way too dark for that and Adrian felt completely alone for the first time ever. At least he was a divine human and he was a God amongst all the other creatures in the galaxy so he would be fine.

Then the wind just stopped and it looked like there was a person on fire in the distance.

Adrian went over to the person. As soon as Adrian saw the poor innocent human on the ground he felt sorry for the man. His flesh was charred, smouldering and deeply damaged.

But the deep dark deep sapphire eyes were okay and they just focused on him.

"Are you the one I sent myself in the future?" the man asked.

Adrian had no idea but it was clear the evil Keres had done this to the poor, innocent human. This was why they had to die and be wiped out.

"I can sense your hate, your ignorance and your humanity," the man said. "Yes, you are the man I sent from the future. Interesting I thought humans would be a little taller,"

"What are you?" Adrian asked wanting to return to Earth immediately to ask the Rex to annihilate the Keres forever.

"I am Geneitor," the man said, "or what is left of him. I am sorry but if I survived in the future then it means I kill you in a few moments. Don't be scared. It isn't that painful, just a little learning process first of all,"

Adrian went to run away but he screamed in agony as he felt the man chomp into his legs. Shattering bones and ripping out chunks of his flesh.

"Tasty," Geneitor said. "Do you have a question whilst I finish off your leg?"

Adrian watched in utter horror as Geneitor held his left leg like a chicken drumstick and sucked the blood before chomping on it.

"What the hell is this place?"

"A good question," Geneitor said licking some blood off his hand. "This is about 4 billion years ago. Earth has only just about formed and this is the Aftermath of the War of Divinity,"

Adrian shrugged.

"This is where me and my wife had a war to end all wars, you humans might say. She was all about life and creating it and I was fucked off with her. So I want to kill everything she ever created,"

Adrian shook his head. It was a shame that Geneitor hadn't won the war at least that way the Keres would be dead.

"My wife created the Keres and humans to survive side by side but that wasn't enough for me. I corrupted humanity and made them win for me against my wife and the Keres,"

"Good," Adrian said.

Genitor wiped his mouth again. "Humans are just as stupid now as before because all you people do is hate. You hate the Keres out of fear but actually, they are the creatures keeping you alive,"

"How?" Adrian asked looking away as Geneitor took another chomp on his leg.

"Simple. In the future when I am recovered and when the Keres uncover my relics that will corrupt them. I will start to return to my consciousness then I will whisper lies into the ears of some Keres but a lot of humans about why the Keres have to die,"

"The Human-Keres war? That was all you,"

"That is brilliant to know. At least I know my relics are found and I am successful," Geneitor said. "I'll have to give you a quick death for that alone,"

Adrian shook his head. Damn this alien God.

"Then I will continue to corrupt the Keres and humanity, and of course my wife will have plans laid too. But she was a lot more injured than I was so I will return first and then my job will simply be to hunt down and kill whatever Cult springs up to resurrect Genetrix,"

"What happens if you fail?" Adrian asked.

Geneitor laughed as his crackling, charred body stood up and looked at Adrian like he was a tasty piece of meat.

"I will not fail. Genetrix will not be resurrected and then finally the Keres, my wife and humanity will all die. Then I will move onto another galaxy and then I will repeat everything again. All life must die and you must die so I can escape into Ultraspace and sleep until my Cult finds me,"

"No," Adrian said as Geneitor unleashed his death magic on him.

And as he died Adrian could only focus on the sheer stupidity of humanity because it wasn't the Keres manipulating humanity, it was a God they didn't believe in.

It was even worse that Adrian couldn't tell anyone because he would die billions of years into a past humanity didn't even know existed because the Rex had outlawed history. Something else he guessed Geneitor had made him do.

And something Adrian was going to regret enforcing forever.

CONNOR WHITELEY

AUTHOR OF AGENTS OF THE EMPEROR SERIES

CREATING ITHANE

A SCIENCE FICTION FAR FUTURE SHORT STORY

CREATING ITHANE

This single event changed the galaxy forever and had the power to doom, save or kill all life.

When people normally say they used to be great, be something or even remotely important, they're lying. They really are. When I was in the Imperial Army fighting on a particularly hard world to pronounce (not that it matters now that it's a lifeless husk), I knew a man that claimed to be a billionaire, the best friend of the glorious Rex and even an inventor.

After spending three years with him in infected mud trenches fighting an enemy he couldn't even understand, I quickly realised that he was a liar, a nobody, a person who was useless and always doomed to die.

You see my name is Ianthe Veilwalker. I don't know why my surname is so weird and futuristic but it works and my parents loved me even as the laser blasts from their Imperial Masters cooked their brains alive. And I did have a good childhood and even when I was serving the Rex in the army I always fought to protect humanity.

That's how I ended up here.

I sat in one of the two corners of my black crystal prison cell that was barely tall enough for me to stand up in. It wasn't wide enough for me to do three steps in any direction and my legs were hardly short.

The entire prison cell was tiny and stunk of blood, corruption and charred flesh so I knew I wasn't the first human to be trapped here.

I had to admit that I really did like the small black crystal dome at the very top of my cell. I didn't doubt for a moment it was what my alien captors were using to watch me. The Dark Keres, the foul humanoid alien race that wanted to resurrect their God of Death, always liked to watch me.

I sort of got the sense that they feared me for some reason and they wanted me dead at all cost, and yet they hadn't tried to kill me just yet. It was weird and strange and I was glad they were next to useless at trying to kill me.

But today felt different.

It wasn't the normal hum, pop and vibration of the air that I now understood to be the life-saving magic that kept the Dark Keres and myself alive. But I felt like someone or something else was watching me and focusing on me like I was about to be picked for something I didn't understand.

Granted I could have just been going mad in this tiny damn prison cell, but that was how the Dark Keres won their psychological wars without even lifting up one of their magical fingers.

You see I had just decided that the Rex was a complete and utter dickhead that only cared about himself and corruption so I went rogue. Me and my squad mates decided to go wrong but the Dark Keres attacked us in our white pod-like shuttle.

We all tried to fight as much as we could but it was useless. The Dark Keres ambushed us and there was nothing we could even remotely do to save ourselves.

I was the only survivor and that was how I ended up in a damn prison cell waiting to die a death that I hoped would come soon. I love humanity, I love life and I want to protect humanity no matter the cost but being in a prison cell just isn't how I want to live.

Someone laughed behind me.

I stood up and noticed how one of the dark crystal walls that trapped me had turned see-through. I stared at the foul, awful Dark Keres with their almost translucent skin, humanoid features and burnt red veins that made him look like a demon.

He smiled at me but I could tell there was no warmth, interest or concern behind those eyes. There was only a lust for murder and pain and my death.

I instantly knew that it was my time to die but knowing the Keres they were certainly not going to make it boring at all.

As the Dark Keres clicked his fingers I felt a fog come over my mind and I collapsed to the ground as my world turned black.

Little did Ianthe know that on the other side of the galaxy a ritual was happening that would change her life and the fate of the galaxy forever.

***

I woke a few moments later and frowned as I found myself in the middle of a massive Colosseum made from the same awful black crystal as my prison cell. It was perfectly smooth, glassy and I just wanted to smash it up, ideally with the skull of a Dark Keres but all I could focus on was the strange ambition of escape.

The Colosseum was immense and I tried to focus on the thousands upon thousands of Dark Keres with their pale skin, awful humanoid features and deranged looks as they focused on me. But I could feel their dark magical energy crackling in the air.

I covered my nose as the air was filled with the horrid aroma of charred flesh, burnt ozone and another more alien smell that I really didn't want to identify.

I had always known that the Dark Keres loved playing games in their Colosseums, and this warband had to be powerful in their hierarchy if they had a Colosseum, but I could feel fear in the air too.

I flat out did not understand how I was now feeling things because this made no sense. I was a normal human woman that wanted to protect, treasure and love life but this ability to actually sense things was just weird.

"See what is about you woman," someone said in a deranged voice.

I shook my head as three human corpses appeared around me

that hadn't been there moments ago. They were all former soldiers like me and they had been completely stripped of armour, weapons and skin as their corpses laid there.

At least I now knew how the Dark Keres dealt with their criminals. They simply killed them in the Colosseums, and the bastards used this for sport and entertainment too. They really were monsters.

"Let us give the Dark Lord Geneitor," someone said, "a game to remember,"

I instantly broke out into a fighting position as I felt the ground vibrate and then a very tall Dark Keres woman appeared. Her white skin glowed dark and magical energy crackled around her.

She had to be a Keres witch corrupted by their God Geneitor to be a mindless instrument of his will.

I so badly wished I had a weapon.

The woman shot out her hands.

Black torrents of fire rushed towards me.

I rolled to one side.

The fire chased me.

The fire turned into dogs.

The dogs chased me.

I ran.

I couldn't allow the fire to touch me.

The witch unleashed more fire.

More dogs formed.

Twenty dogs chased me.

I spun around.

I had to fight death with life.

I charged.

The dogs hesitated.

I didn't.

I leapt into the air.

Kicking a fiery dog in the head.

It died.

Agony shot through my leg.

The dogs charged at me.

I punched them.

Kicked them.

Snapped their bones.

My skin burnt.

My clothes fused to my skin.

The witch made a black fiery sword form in her hand.

She flew at me.

She swung.

Again.

And again.

I ducked.

I rolled.

I fled.

Black magical energy gripped a hold of me.

Throwing me towards her.

I flew towards the witch.

She raised her sword. I grabbed it as I slammed into her.

I thrusted it into her. The witch died.

As soon as the witch's corpse disappeared, the entire damn Colosseum went deadly silent and they all looked to a particular point that I couldn't see. Maybe they wanted to ask their warlord what was going to happen next. Maybe they might give me my freedom.

I seriously doubted it.

"Most impressive human," someone said, "but let us see how you do against the most devout servants of Geneitor,"

I shook my head. "All I want is to live. Protect life. Save people. That is all I want so I don't want to kill you,"

I didn't know why I said that but it just felt right in the moment. But as a massive wolf the size of a shuttle appeared at the other end of the Colosseum I seriously knew that I could never ever reason with the Dark Keres.

The wolf charged.

I went to roll.

I felt a sword at my feet. The same one the witch had used. I grabbed it.

I charged at the wolf.

The wolf charged even faster.

I jumped into the air.

I swung the sword.

The sword shattered as it touched the wolf.

The Dark Keres laughed.

It was deafening.

The wolf chomped down on my leg.

Throwing me about like a rag doll. Breaking my leg. Shattering bone.

The wolf threw me to one side.

I landed with a thud.

I forced myself up. I couldn't use a leg.

The wolf charged.

I tried to run.

I couldn't.

The wolf whacked me to one side.

I smashed into the black crystal.

The wolf roared.

It was playing with me as it slowly came over to me and I realised that I was going to die here. I was going to become just another victim one of the Dark Keres and my soul or whatever it was called would be tortured and devoured by Geneitor, forever.

It was weird because all I wanted to do was protect people, preserve life and make sure that no one ever harmed an innocent person again.

I stared in utter defiance as the wolf came over to me and grinned with an unnaturally human smile as its fangs got closer.

The wolf snapped me in two.

Everyone cheered, laughed and sang happy songs as the life drained from me but I realised that as everything turned white, that I wasn't actually dead yet.

I saw an immense picture of a Keres woman formed but this woman was kind, angelic and I could feel her sheer aura of life, hope and protection. She was inspiring as hell even though I didn't know her and all she made me want to do was get back to my body and defeat the Dark Keres.

"How badly do you want to protect life human?" the woman asked in perfect Imperial tongue.

"With all my being,"

"Will you serve me and become the Daughter of Genetrix?" the woman asked.

I didn't know what she meant but I knew that Genetrix was the Keres Goddess of life, protection and hope. And if Geneitor was real then she had to be real too.

"Definitely," I said with such rage that I hope she knew how angry I was at the Dark Keres for daring to kill me.

"Then return to life Daughter of Genetrix and free me,"

Before I could ask what she meant I felt pure magical energy pour into me and I was flat out amazed at all the Keres knowledge, forbidden texts and divine guidance that was entering my mind. I might not have known everything about the Keres and their gods but that didn't matter for now.

I opened my eyes back in the Colosseum and I shook my head at the Wolf.

Everyone noticed what was happening as they stopped their cheering, singing and laughing. And let me tell you hearing that deafening noise stop was shocking as hell.

I thrusted out my hand and an immense white lightning bolt shot out that killed the wolf so quickly that I had to double-check that it had actually died.

"What is this?" everyone shouted.

I smiled as I felt the love, guidance and protection of Genetrix flow through my veins. "This is the future Dark Keres. Genetrix has touched my soul, given me power and now I will make sure you fail to resurrect Geneitor and wipe out all life in the galaxy,"

"Impossible," someone said. "Geneitor is all-powerful. He has a cult dedicated to him and we will find all the Soulstones needed to bring him down,"

"You might have a head start on us. You might have the resources that we don't. But I am the Daughter and Chosen of Genetrix and I will not allow you to live any longer,"

"Kill her lads,"

I just grinned as the stupid Dark Keres leapt down over the Colosseum's black crystal railings as they charged towards me. I flicked my wrists and two huge white swords formed in my hands. And I was so glad I had specialised in sword combat back in the Imperial Army.

I charged.

I swung.

I sliced.

I diced.

It was a slaughter.

I ripped into the flesh of the enemy.

Throats were slashed.

Chests exploded.

Dark Keres screamed out in agony.

There were too many. Too many Dark Keres for me to kill. They would overwhelm me in short order.

I fell back.

I sensed the Keres were behind me.

I ducked. A sword passed behind me.

I realised I had to keep killing. Keep fighting. Keep living.

I didn't know how I knew. But each death brought me closer to my salvation because Genetrix would help me.

Yet first she needed death to power her creation.

I screamed in rage.

I dived forward.

Swinging my swords.

Slashing throats in bloody arcs.
Ramming my swords into chests.
Unleashing torrents of fire with my mind.
A sword slashed my back.
I froze.
The Dark Keres sliced my arms.
I dropped my swords.
The Keres kicked me to the ground.
They jumped on my head.
I screamed in crippling pain.
I unleashed a fireball.
Killing two Keres.
And that was when it happened.

I felt the veil between this reality and the next become paper thin and then they disappeared.

"Come to me Vita," I said.

An immense deafening roar, scream and shout in a language I didn't know all rolled into one echoed across the planet as a blinding white light appeared above me.

Vita was a demon, a demi-God, a creation by divine power that I could summon and I was more than glad about that.

She was a huge Keres woman with golden magical energy crackling around her.

She screamed out. She launched torrents of white fire. She unleashed all her divine power.

The Dark Keres didn't stand a chance as Vita slaughtered them. The Keres tried to run, tried to flee, tried to scream. It didn't matter as Vita cooked them alive, slaughtered them and scooped up their souls so Genetrix could protect them against the predations of Geneitor.

Within a few moments the slaughter was over and Vita just smiled at me, and I wasn't sure if this was Vita smiling or Genetrix. Maybe she was impressed with what I had done, maybe she was pleased to see her Will made real for a change or maybe she was happy that there was now hope in the galaxy that Geneitor and the Dark Keres might not win after all.

I didn't know what had caused this at all. I didn't know why Genetrix had decided on me as the perfect human or living creature for that now, to become part of her. But I didn't care because for the first time in my life, I actually felt like I had a purpose.

I had always been interested and dedicated to protecting, saving and helping to preserve life and now with Genetrix's power I had the ability to do it. So I bowed to Vita as she disappeared and then it was just me left in the darkness of a former Dark Keres world.

But there was a single rose that grew out of the ground, and that really did make me smile. It showed that even in the most deadly of places, life could and would endure and considering the thousands of Imperial worlds that had been rendered lifeless husks by the Rex's pointless wars, that gave me a hell of a lot of hope for the future.

A future I might not have been certain about, but a future I was really, really excited about because I was Ianthe Veilwalker, human and Daughter of Genetrix.

It was my job to stop the Dark Keres from resurrecting Geneitor no matter the cost.

And that meant the entire galaxy depended on me.

AUTHOR OF AGENTS OF THE EMPEROR SERIES

CONNOR WHITELEY

RITUAL OF REBIRTH

A SCIENCE FICTION FAR FUTURE SHORT STORY

RITUAL OF REBIRTH

After fighting to protect humanity on hundreds of worlds, after killing more enemies than he cared to remember and after being betrayed by more people than he wanted to think about, Commander Jerico Nelson had never ever expected to be in the employ of the very alien race that he had unfortunately killed out of blind obedience to humanity's monstrous leader known as the Rex.

Jerico wasn't particularly a fan of this strategic position as he stood on the very edge of a massive blood-red crater with gentle slopes. The slopes alone with its near perfectly smooth red rocks made this a bad position to defend. Ideally he would have loved to be in a crater with steep slopes that would slow down the enemies. Yet these awful red slopes wouldn't do anything to make his defence job any easier.

The entire red, sandy, rocky planet wasn't ideal for defence. Jerico wasn't a fan of the massive red mountains in the distance that rose up from the ground like daggers, just waiting to kill him, his men and his alien allies.

He really loved positions that were surrounded by flat ground so he could see his enemies for miles before they actually got within striking distance. But he couldn't help his stomach tighten at the very notion of snipers setting up in the mountains to take him and his men out.

The only major benefit of this crater that was there was a small rocky platform that his alien allies, the Keres, had created for him and his men. At least that way if there was an attack then they could easily hide, jump down and use it as their own snipers' nest.

But Jerico just couldn't help focusing on the stormy sky above them. The blood-red clouds with small amounts of crimson swirled in them really didn't make Jerico feel at ease. The gathering storm looked evil, cold and like it was going to be the death of all of them.

The entire planet smelt of damp sand with the odd hint of gun oil, burnt ozone and charred sage from the ritual that the Keres were hoping to perform in the crater. That made the great taste of roast dinner form on his tongue.

Jerico stepped down onto the rocky platform where the five remaining squad mates of his were all playing cards in their black battle armour. They were smiling, having fun and acting like there wasn't a single danger in the galaxy.

Granted Jerico didn't know if the ritual was going to be attacked. He was simply wanting to be sure because the Keres, or as this cult preferred to be called the Daughter of Genetrix, were paying a lot of Rexes for the job.

He still didn't understand how none of the Keres fractions had any sort of currency and their society was based on need and mutual respect. But these Keres were nice, kind and helpful so Jerico didn't mind not understanding everything about them.

Jerico looked down at the bottom of the crater and just shook his head. The Keres were wearing some kind of strange bright white robe that made them look even more like elves and fairies, because of their pointy features, unnaturally thin humanoid body and their almond-shaped eyes.

They had to be finishing up the preparations because Jerico noticed there were the five red, blue and purple Soul stones that the Keres had been obsessed with for months. Apparently each of the Soul Stones contained a Demi-god belonging to their Goddess of Life Genetrix.

Jerico didn't buy it.

But the Rexes were good and he really wanted to upgrade his

equipment and actually pay his men so he really, really didn't care.

"Commander we are ready," a Keres said in a scarily good impression of Imperial Tongue.

Jerico nodded and he tightened his grip on his machine gun and he gestured that his men should also start to get ready, because if an attack was going to happen then it was going to happen very, very soon.

Jerico watched his men go up to the top of the ridge of the crater and he was about to join them when he caught what was happening with the Keres below.

All of them were holding hands and sitting on the icy cold floor with sharp shards of rock digging into their asses. The five Soul stones were in the middle and they were glowing.

The Keres started singing a beautifully sweet perfect melody that made Jerico want to cry, something he hadn't done in decades and he felt the air crackle, buzz and hum with magical energy around him.

Jerico looked up and frowned as the thunder roared overhead. The violent storm clouds were coming together and Jerico had a very, very bad feeling about this.

It got even worse when an immense spherical warship belonging to the Rex appeared in-between flashes of lightning.

The Imperium was here and they were going to attack.

Jerico went to shout to the Keres but his mouth was frozen and he felt like something was influencing him not to interfere under any circumstances. And for some reason he obeyed.

He rushed up to the top with the rest of his men.

"We have company," Jerico said.

He nodded at Thomas as he checked his pistols and young Allen looked unsure about his third battle but Jerico had faith in all of his men.

A deafening roar screamed overhead as a nuclear bomb was dropped.

Jerico wanted to scream like the rest of his men but he knew they would be okay for now. The Goddess Genetrix would protect them and as soon as the nuclear bomb touched the top of an invisible dome the sheer extreme impact was reflected.

Jerico's mouth dropped as he saw the sheer destructive power of the bomb rip the Imperial vessel limb from limb.

A Keres screamed in agony.

The storm clouds smashed into each other.

The thunder roared.

It screamed.

It screamed bloody murder.

Jerico's ears started to bleed.

Black lightning shot down around them.

Jerico jumped to one side.

The ritual was starting now and Jerico knew that it flat out couldn't be undone. Something was happening not in this reality but Jerico understood in a way he didn't understand that his life was about to change forever.

A furious roar echoed around the planet as Jerico saw two white pod-like shuttles were flying towards them. Some damn humans from the Imperial ship had survived.

Jerico clocked that the two shuttles were splitting up.

Jerico grabbed Thomas and Allen and he took them to the other side of the crater.

The shuttle landed with a crash and Jerico aimed his gun at the door of the pod-like shuttle. He wanted, needed to kill these humans to protect whatever was going on.

The shuttle doors exploded open.

The Imperial army soldiers exploded out.

Firing as they went.

Jerico fired back.

Bullets slammed into Jerico's armour.

He stood firm. He couldn't be defeated.

He fired controlled shots.

Bullets screamed through the air.

Smashing into the enemy's faces.

Heads exploded.

Skulls shattered.

Thomas's head imploded.

Jerico ran backwards.

More high-velocity shots screamed at him.

Jerico spun around.

There were snipers in the mountains.

Jerico ran over the ridge of the crater with Allen.

They charged at the soldiers.

Cutting them down.

Jerico unleashed the full power of his gun.

He slaughtered the enemy.

The shuttle exploded.

Throwing them forward.

Jerico slowly forced himself up and he was so glad that he was okay. All the enemies in the shuttle were dead and that him and Allen could now go and reinforce the other position but the storm screamed in terror overhead.

Jerico looked over to Allen's unmoving body and he went over to it. Allen's eyes were glassy and cold and lifeless as Jerico noticed all the metal shards from the shuttle covered his body.

The storm roared overhead.

The wind was howling all around him creating immense sandstorms.

Jerico could barely see where he was going so he allowed his instincts to guide him.

He made his way round the crater but he was annoyed as hell he could no longer hear the gunshots and screaming of the Imperial soldiers. He really hoped that his men were okay.

He couldn't lose them. They had to live. Just had to.

Jerico found his way to the other side and he frowned at the three remaining dead bodies of his men. The other Imperial shuttle had exploded and the mountain in the distance shattered as a lightning bolt from the storm smashed into it.

"Help Genetrix!" a Keres shouted at the top of her lungs.

The storm grew even more intense.

Jerico ran up the crater.

Lightning bolts hammered the ground.

Jerico leapt to one side.

Then another.

Then another.

Lightning bolts were everywhere.

Immense chunks of mountain rock fell down around him.

Jerico ran away from the crater.

The chunks of rock hammered the ground.

And then Jerico went down the crater as fast as he could but he already knew it was way, way too late to save anyone.

As the storm screamed a final time and unleashed vast amounts of magical energy into the atmosphere that scorched Jerico's lungs and made him scream out in agony, Jerico collapsed to his knees as he saw what the hell had happened.

All the Soul Stones were gone now and where they had once been was littered with the corpses of humans and Keres alike. A lot of the rock inside the crater was charred and smouldering so Jerico had no idea what had caused that.

But he had failed.

It was Jerico's job to protect his men, protect the Keres and make sure that whatever had happened today was going to happen without a single problem. He was nothing but a failure.

Jerico had no idea how he was going to contact the families, friends and loved ones of his proud wonderful men that had died under his command. He couldn't tell the families any of the details because it was illegal for humans to work with the Keres but he wanted to help the victims of this attack somehow.

Jerico saw something move below him.

Jerico slowly went down into the crater with his machine gun ready to fire if needed. The entire crater smelt awful of charred flesh, burnt ozone and another strange burnt smell that was probably to do with the sheer amount of magic in the air.

"You live," a female Keres said in her blood soaked and blackened robes.

Jerico rushed over to her and held her in his arms. He applied pressure to the wound but it was still flowing too quickly. She was going to die and it would be all his fault.

"I'm sorry I failed," Jerico said.

The woman laughed. "You did not fail Son of Genetrix. This outcome was already predetermined by the Goddess and this has the potential to save or doom all life in the galaxy,"

"I don't understand,"

"Humans never do," the woman said. "The Goddess works in magical ways. She came to me with the last of her power a century ago so I could find the Soulstones and Rebirth her so she may walk amongst the stars like she did millions of years ago,"

"But I failed you," Jerico said.

"This is not the right time for Genetrix to return," the woman said. "And now know that I was not the one to Rebirth her. There is a human woman called Ithane Veilwalker, she is the true Daughter of Genetrix,"

Jerico wasn't sure. Why the hell would a Keres Goddess want to have a mere human as her chosen.

"You must find her, protect her and keep her safe. She has just been reborn herself and you must find her. It is only through her that Geneitor is defeated and life in the galaxy will continue. Will you do that for me?"

Jerico nodded because he flat out hated the feeling of her warm blood oozing all over his hands as he failed yet again to save her life.

"Good," the woman said grinning. "Then take my necklace too. The Goddess was clever and she showed me the way. Take the necklace and may the Soulstone of Spero, Goddess of Hope, guide you like it has me,"

Jerico was about to question it. He couldn't be entrusted with such an important task, he was a failure, he was nothing, he was a mere human. But the female Keres died in his arms and he simply took off the golden necklace with the weird blue crystal at the end of it, and smiled.

He had no idea what the future was going to offer. The future could have been dark horrid and filled with suffering for all he knew but he had his mission and he had his destiny already laid out for him.

He wasn't sure that any human truly understood what intergalactic and maybe even interdimensional game of God and Goddess they were all blindly entering into, but that didn't matter. Because he was going to find this Ithane woman, he was going to find the Soulstones once more and he was going to succeed this time.

And bring down Geneitor once and for all.

All because he had hope for a better future, a better life and hopefully redemption for allowing all the amazing people around him to die, when they really didn't need to.

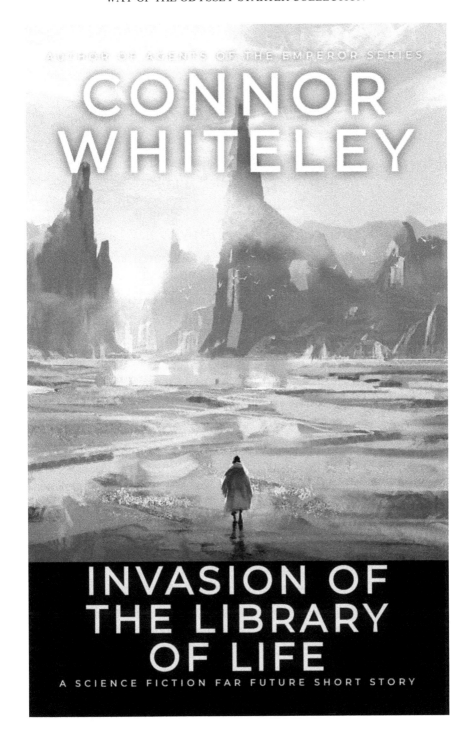

INVASION OF THE LIBRARY OF LIFE

The thick aroma of smoke, charred flesh and death clung to the air as I leant against the icy cold white marble railing of the balcony I was using as my position. I, Ithane Veilwalker, enjoyed the small amounts of coldness flowing up my arms and into my soul.

The entire balcony itself was rather good for watching the surrounding forests considering it was a wide semi-circular marble platform used for academics, readers and other scholars. In normal times they would have read out here and studied their texts and ancient books in the bright sunlight.

That wasn't happening anymore.

I was completely alone on the balcony today and there weren't even any small crystal tables or chairs that had covered the balcony when I had first arrived a few days ago. There were still the little cuts, slices and chips in the floor where people had removed the tables and chairs, but they were so minor it hardly mattered.

The entire tower, or Library of Life as it was called by the locals, was a place I had always wanted to visit. The entire tower was created and handcrafted from a solid immense block of beautiful white marble with stunning gold veining coursing through it like a river.

I was even more impressed with the thousands of ancient leather-bound books that lined the white shiny shelves inside. I had never seen a real book before, most of them had been burnt and annihilated when the evil Rex had risen to power and conquered the Imperium.

Books really were special things to all of us remaining humans because we knew the key to our freedom and saving humanity was written in our past. The past that was burning down around us.

I smiled to myself as the taste of barbeques formed my tongue, my parents had always liked them with my siblings and our large family. They might have been all dead now but they had given me an amazing childhood.

A massive roar ripped through the air and I just shook my head as a bright red missile flashed through the sky smashing into the immense forest in the distance.

The sky was veiled in smoke, ash and little white pods called shuttles. I knew exactly why the Imperium was invading this world and killing my friends. They wanted to kill me and see what I knew about the Mother of Life.

I never realised that being resurrected by an alien goddess and being made into her Will incarnate would make me so popular with the monsters of the galaxy. But Genetrix wanted me on this world and thankfully I had a friend translating an ancient text for me now.

I felt Genetrix pull on my mind a little and I knew that I was running out of time. The Imperium would breach the world's defenders soon enough and then they would kill me and the knowledge of the text would be lost forever.

Of course I could easily open a portal and just leave but the text was too fragile to move and my damn translator wouldn't leave this planet. Some rubbish about their soul being bound to the world, I hated how magic worked at times.

"My Lady," someone said behind me.

I rolled my eyes as a Keres man came up to me. His alien humanoid features were perfectly thin, a little gaul and elongated. His body looked way too thin for a human but that was so common amongst the Keres.

Genetrix might have created the Keres to protect life and her evil husband might have created humanity to kill all life but they were basically the same in the looks department.

"Yes Tau'Koo," I said feeling Genetrix really trying to pull on my mind. There was something the Goddess wanted me to realise but I just couldn't understand at the moment.

"The orbital defences are wiped out and the ground defenders are weaker now. The Imperium has landed in the North and South of the planet and Keres lives are being slaughtered,"

"Damn it," I said. I might have been 100% human with the powers of a Keres but I had never wanted the Keres to die. They were good, amazing people that had to be protected, but my presence had brought the enemy to them.

I needed a new plan.

"How much longer does the Translator need?" I asked.

"Another twenty minutes at least but which-"

I waved him silent because I knew exactly what was going to happen in the next twenty minutes, this world was going to die.

"Then let us see what power the Mother can gift me," I said closing my eyes and connecting to Genetrix and letting her presence feel my mind.

I tapped into her power and started to course over the immense forest below me with my mind's eye like how a bird might fly towards a seed on the ground. I needed to find the leader of the invasion and I needed to buy us time.

I found him.

I connected with his mind instantly. He wasn't a good man by any stretch of the imagination but he was skilled in hunting, killing and torturing Keres. I didn't need alien magic to realise that because I could sense the crystallised magic of his former kills.

Even now I was surprised that if the Keres were tortured for long enough their bodies would discharge their magic and connection to their patron God in an effort to save their life. It never worked but it didn't stop the biological processes of the Keres from doing it.

"I see you monster," I said echoing the words into his mind and hoping I could force a reaction of some kind.

I felt his thoughts turn happy that he actually wanted this and he had been expecting this.

"Where are you abomination?" he asked, "and tell me, what thoughts can you see?"

I didn't like it how he knew about the mind-reading ability Genetrix had gifted me. There had to be a spy amongst my gang and that was a major problem.

I didn't stop though, I could see his past and abuse from the family that was meant to love him. I could see how the Keres had robbed him of the chance to ever see if his parents could love him (they never were going to but he didn't realise that) and I could see his name.

He was Bloodheart.

The name almost forced me to kill the connection. Everyone in the galaxy knew who Bloodheart was, I wasn't even sure he was real or just a myth to keep the Imperium scared. He was a murderer, a butcherer and capable of burning an entire planet for the fun of the killing.

I only needed another 15 minutes.

"You are an impressive name to find Bloodheart," I said feeling Genetrix wanting me to leave.

But I couldn't. I could face Bloodheart.

"Do you realise that you are not the only human touched by the Keres Gods?" he asked. "There is another one of you and he is strong, deadly and will kill all life in this galaxy,"

I killed the connection as I felt something stand behind me.

I instantly went for the long magical sword at my waist but I felt a hard knife press against my back.

"Tau'koo," I said hardly impressed that the damn bastard actually had a blade at me.

"There are many within your ranks that do not agree having a human as the leader of the Daughters of Genetrix," Tau'Koo said.

I laughed because he was no Daughter of the Goddess, even I could hear the death, corruption and sickness in his voice. He was not devoted to life, he was the Deathbringer, a servant of Geneitor.

"When did the Father corrupt you?" I asked knowing I could kill him at a moment's notice but I just needed answers.

Immense booms ripped through the air. Huge red flashes raced across the sky.

More missiles rained down on the planet. As did ten thousand little white pods. The ground forces were going to be overwhelmed in moments.

"The Father did not corrupt me. He showed me the truth about the galaxy and how humanity must die, the Keres must die, everyone must die,"

I snapped his neck with a single thought and whipped out my longsword as I went back into the immense library of Life. I was running out of time and I needed my answers.

I went along a narrow marble corridor with thousands of blue leather-bound books lining the shelves. None of them had been touched in decades but the hope of a better life and the magic within the pages kept the dust off them. Hope was a very powerful force in the galaxy.

After a few moments of going along the corridor, I just grinned as I ducked into a small white marble chamber through a small archway. There was a heavy wooden desk in the middle but my translator was dead.

Their body lumped over the damn desk and the ancient text was damaged.

I placed my hands on the translator's forehead, it was still warm and I hated the weird feeling of a warm dead body. It was wrong on so many levels.

"Let me see what never should be seen Mother of Life," I said quietly.

My mind was filled with curiosity, love and happiness as I entered the translator's last final moments. At least they were happy with their last task for the Mother. They were reading a passage about a Soulstone and they were murdered.

I shook my head because it was the Soulstones I was after.

Whoever collected all five shards of Genetrix's being could resurrect her and then she could finally kill her husband once and for all. It was simple and I needed to find all the Soulstones.

I sadly had to push my friend's corpse off the ancient book and their body turned to ash and I clicked my fingers so their soul went to the Mother instead of being tortured by the Father.

There was a bloody fingerprint highlighting one particular section and I couldn't read it. The language made no sense to me because I was a human, not a Keres and I didn't understand long lost languages.

But there was still a little bit of hope.

An immense boom ripped through the library and it sounded like a thousand tons of marble had just come smashing down.

I was seriously running out of time but the preservation of all life in the galaxy was more important than my single life.

I closed my eyes and tried to reconnect with the translator's passing soul but I couldn't. Once a soul was given to Genetrix she kept an iron grip on it.

I just couldn't help but laugh because this was so stupid and I couldn't possibly fail but Bloodheart was coming here. And I had seen in his mind when I connected only moments ago, he knew the ancient language and he knew exactly what I wanted with the Library.

"Return to me Bloodheart," I said as I reconnected with his mind.

I almost jumped as I didn't expect his mind to actually be in the Library. He was here stalking the halls and killing the Keres defenders as he went.

"I was waiting for you," he said, "because I wanted to show you a party trick,"

I screamed in agony as I was pulled through reality and dropped off in front of Bloodheart as him and me were completely alone in the ruined remains of a library.

The white marble walls were smashed and the smoke-veiled sky could easily be seen through the immense holes in the ceiling. There were plenty of Keres corpses littering the ground and I wanted to slaughter him right there and then.

There were even a few smashed marble pillars lining the edges of the library.

Bloodheart in his heavy, thick metal armour pointed his sword at my chest and aimed a pistol at my head.

I went a little cold as I felt my connection with Genetrix fade a little and I just realised that Bloodheart was a son of Geneitor. I had no idea how a human had fallen to the corruption but I was still so new at this.

"You will regret your choice of Patron," Bloodheart said. "The Father kills and he will enjoy you,"

"I regret nothing but why this world? I have been the Daughter of Genetrix for three months now. You have not attacked me in the void, on Ferum or five different worlds. Why this one?"

"Because this world has Keres on it. I love snapping the necks of the Keres as they sleep,"

"You are a monster," I said.

"I am what the galaxy has created me and I will help the Rex rule the stars in Humanity's name. No more Keres, no aliens, no more anything,"

I gasped for a moment as I realised Geneitor didn't have full control over him yet because Bloodheart still wanted humanity to live even though he had said the opposite only moments ago.

Bloodheart still had the weakness and mortality of a human.

He charged.

I thrusted out my hands.

Unleashing torrents of fire.

He flicked a wrist. My torrents went away.

He leapt into the air. Kicking me in the chest.

I fell backwards on the ground.

He landed on me. Kicking me again. Again.

The smell of death, smoke and rotting flesh filled my senses.

I shot out my hands.

Sending him backwards.
I shot up.
I flew at him.
Launching fireball after fireball.
He hissed.
He charged.
I charged.
We raised our swords.
We swung.
Our blades met.
Immense red flashes lit up the sky.
A missile screamed towards us.
I shot out another fireball.
Bloodheart hissed.
The missile smashed down on us.

I slammed my sword into the ground as the missile's explosive power was unleashed, I focused on my love for life, protecting the innocent and hope and a thin shield of dazzling white magical energy formed around me.

Bright flashes of gold, red and orange screamed past me as the deafening roar of an entire building collapsing echoed around me. I had failed the Mother, the Keres and ultimately humanity.

When the collapsing and the fire stopped, I closed my eyes and portalled myself to the top of the ruins where I simply sat on top of the very, very warm marble rubble. I didn't like how it was almost burning my bum but I didn't care because I was thankfully alive.

I hated how the sky was black with immense columns of black smoke veiling the sky. The forest was ablaze and all the little white pods were zooming back up into orbit because they had done their mission and I didn't doubt for a second that Bloodheart was alive.

The only sound of the entire planet now was the constant roaring, crackling and snapping of fires as they devoured all in their path. If there were members of the Dark Keres Cult on the planet then I wouldn't have been surprised if Geneitor was powering the life-destroying flames but thankfully they weren't here.

I just shook my head as I couldn't believe I had completely failed in my mission, then I felt my connection to the Mother restore itself and it felt happy.

A strange joy filled me as I realised that I wasn't just a human now constrained by the limits of a human mind. I was also a Keres with the power of a Goddess behind me, and I started to remember little passages and shards of information from the section of ancient text I had been reading earlier, that was all me.

But I understood it now and I just laughed as I realised my magic must have coursed its way through Bloodheart's mind when we were fighting and it must have found where he kept all his information about the Keres ancient language.

The passage the Translator wanted me to understand was that the Soulstones might have been bought together at one point in history. It was after all the ritual that tried to resurrect Genetrix failing at the same exact time as my own death that brought around my creation.

It was still more than that though, the book was mentioning how the Soulstones never wanted to be apart from each other and they wanted to be found. They would influence the environments, the worlds, the cultures that surrounded them so someone would eventually notice something was seriously wrong in a good or bad way.

I just shook my head because this was basically asking me to understand how the Soulstones had been discovered in the first place and then I could look for similar signs in the present. But the galaxy was a massive place, filled with billions of different planets and a Soulstone could be on any one of them.

I stood up and took a final look at this now-dead world I could sense that a darkness was coming here. Geneitor had a world to consume and he had a lot of dead souls to collect, but I was never going to allow him that for I might be a human but I am Ithane Veilwalker, Daughter of Genetrix and I am a protector of life.

I clicked my fingers and felt my connection with Genetrix strengthen as I collected all the souls on the planets and gifted them to her.

Then I swirled, twirled and whirled my arms about and I opened a bright golden portal to my flagship with my cult. I had a lot of reading to do, a lot of learning and a lot of things to think about because I was making progress and that was a wonderful feeling to have.

One day Genetrix would rise once more and then the entire galaxy would know the meaning of life and death. And only one side would win forever.

DEATH OF A FAMILIAR

AUTHOR OF AGENTS OF THE EMPEROR SERIES

CONNOR WHITELEY

A SCIENCE FICTION FAR FUTURE SHORT STORY

DEATH OF A FAMILIAR

Today taught me why humans couldn't be trusted because this was the day I died for my Goddess.

The last thing I would ever call humans is normal. They are strange, complex and very smelly creatures with their soft flesh, large waists and they are just weird to look at.

I had met many humans over my long life on many worlds that I mostly forget now, but the story of humanity and their species is all the same. War, killing and blind ignorance of the truth about the universe.

And I should know to be honest because as I curl up in my wonderfully soft purple Familiar bed, that a bastard human had once decided to call a "cat bed" as if I was such a low life as a cat. I was a Familiar of the Keres race, a cat-like creature with much more beautiful, softer and striking purple fur given life by the Goddess Genetrix herself. I was not a cat.

But yet I digress, my apologies.

You see I was all nice and toasty and curled up on my bed, allowing the wonderful warmth that my magic pulsed into the velvet fabric, to travel back into me. It was like sitting on a warm metal chair without the intensity of the heat. I loved it.

I rested my little head on the edge of the bed and stared out at my boss's new room that was oddly human and I hated it. considering my boss was a Keres, a much thinner, pure and magical version of humanity created by the Goddess of Life Genetrix millions of years ago, I didn't understand the human decorations.

The office itself was a massive grey metal box in my opinion with weird orbs of bright white golden light floating near the dark grey ceiling. The little orbs were pretty to look at as they bounced along the ceiling causing shadows to dance across the grey floor.

The entire office just looked cold and isolated and not Keres at all. I had always loved the wonderfully dark purple, red and blue crystals that the Keres manipulated to create whatever their impressive minds could develop. By contrast human design just always felt a little lacking.

My boss was sitting at her ugly massive desk that was an immense slab of grey metal with some cute Keres items on them. I noticed she had a glass bowl of blue glowing crystals that she had placed a magical shield over to stop me devouring all those delicious treats at once.

She was crafty like that.

But I could sense my boss was tense, nervous and her single claw tapped loudly against the metal desk.

She had developed that clawed finger way before I was gifted to her by the Goddess but it had apparently happened during a spell gone wrong. She had wanted to cast a torrent of fire at some humans that were going to kill some innocent people but the spell backfired.

She tried to focus too much magic through a single finger so the finger exploded, killed the humans and saved the innocent but the finger had twisted into a claw.

A cold, dead, awful-looking claw.

"Do you sense the humans yet?" my boss asked me.

I wasn't even sure why my boss wanted to see a whole bunch of smelly humans today in this awful office. Even the hints of human coffee, caramel and toffee that stunk out the air was out of place and I might have been lending my magic to create the smell but it was still out of place.

The only benefit was the great taste of toffee that formed on my tongue. I did enjoy it when humans brought me treats like that.

"Tazzie," my boss said, "do you sense the humans?"

I closed my eyes briefly and coursed my magic through the immense crystal-like ship we were currently on. The banging, humming and popping of the ship tried to interfere with my senses but it failed.

I felt the darkness of the Death God Geneitor press against my mind but I couldn't allow the Great Enemy to stop me. I coursed my magic through the entire ship and then I detected the dull glow of human souls boarding.

"Of course," I said almost offended my boss actually believed I wouldn't be able to. "I still do not understand the importance of seeing the humans in *this* place,"

My boss stood up and I admired her long blond golden hair that framed her sharp, pointed face and ears perfectly.

"These humans are not from the Imperium and they do not serve the Rex. They could be allies in the fight to save the Keres,"

I didn't bother moving my head because I was comfortable and enjoying the warmth far too much to risk moving. But I still rolled my eyes.

I really did like my boss and I was grateful for the Goddess to gift me to her, but she was an idiot at times. The tyrannical awful Imperium and that monstrous Rex, their leader, would hunt down every single element of the Keres they couldn't manipulate or control. And then one day they would want to wipe us all out.

It was simply the truth.

The Death God wanted to obliterate Genetrix's creations and he was using humanity to do it. Yet because humanity refused to believe in the simple truth that the two divine beings existed, they were walking themselves further and further into damnation with each passing day.

I doubt these humans would be any different.

"You doubt me?" my boss said.

I grinned and tried to hide my fang-like teeth from her. "Of course I doubt you. I doubt your entire race at times because of what you allowed to happen and continues to happen,"

My boss stood up perfectly straight as we both realised the humans were coming closer to the office.

"The main Keres race might be happy living by the monstrous terms of the Treaty of Defeat that means we're slaves to humanity but I will not allow that. It is why I serve the Goddess as a Daughter of Genetrix,"

I nodded and smiled as the cold metal door of the office hissed open and three humans walked in.

I covered my nose with a purple paw as the foul aroma of sweat, blood and human waste filled the air. I am sure they wouldn't have smelt to other humans but I was a Familiar and my senses were extreme.

Even my boss didn't seem to notice too much.

Boss clicked her fingers and three very human wooden chairs appeared. I was disgusted in how simple and artless the humans were about their chairs. It was a crime against the beauty that Genetrix placed in the world but I had to behave.

"Who is the cat?" one of the humans asked but at this point they all looked as weird as each other.

"Tazzie is not a cat. She is a Familiar gifted to me by Genetrix, Creator of Life,"

I rolled my eyes and leapt from my bed to the desk making all the humans jump.

I stood there as Boss continued to introduce the mission of the Daughter of Genetrix and how they wanted to protect both the Keres and humanity from the predations of Geneitor.

I rolled my eyes again at the humans but they were all wearing bright baby blue military uniforms and I could sense there was darkness in each of them. It wasn't a massive amount of darkness or even something to be alarmed about, but something wasn't right.

"Why is the Familiar looking at us?" the human to my left asked.

"Her job is threefold. She is meant to protect me, amplify my power and serve Genetrix however she sees fit," Boss said.

I stared at the human. "And sometimes that means killing whoever attacks us,"

The humans smiled like I was some type of domestic play animal that couldn't possibly hurt them.

"We have been sent here by the Enlightened Republic to support you in exchange for you helping us," the tallest human said taking out a something large wrapped in black cloth.

I hissed as soon as I sensed the darkness and Death Magic pouring out of the black cloth.

I flashed my fangs at the humans but again they didn't seem concerned at all. They were more focused on Boss as she hissed and wiped her nose like trying to wipe away a bad smell.

The human placed the object on the desk so I backed away and smiled as even the desk groaned in protest of having something so dark on it.

"So the humans bring us a Death Object," I said through clenched teeth. That had to be a foul crime itself and it was outrageous that the humans had discovered such an object in the first place.

No wonder I had sensed Darkness in them. The mere exposure to such an object would cause Geneitor's influence to take root in their mind, body and soul.

"This is outrageous, Boss," I said. "The Goddess would never allow this object on one of her ships,"

Without warning the humans took off the black cloth and they made sure a small piece of the cloth touched my paw.

The cloth burned my paw and turned the purple fur to ash. I shot backwards hissing in agony.

The air crackled with purple magical energy around me but Boss raised a warning finger at the humans and I knew she would deal with the situation.

Yet I understood why she hadn't killed the humans for now because if there was a Death Object in play then we had to deal with it and find out if the humans were a real threat or not.

I slowly went over to the bowl-like object that had been covered by the cloth and I flat out hated the weird shrieking sound that echoed inside my head. I knew the damn humans wouldn't have been able to hear it, but then again me and Boss were sensitive to this stuff.

In fact every single Keres on the ship was probably hearing this and having the Darkness try to influence and push into their minds, bodies and souls.

I didn't want to have this aboard any longer than needed but there was something weird about the design.

This particular Death Object was a large black bowl made from a strange type of glassy stone with millions of lines of writing. It was clearly Keres writing from the shape but the little black tendrils coming off the bowl made it hard to read.

I wasn't sure if those tendrils were natural or if the Goddess was trying to protect us from the evil writing.

"What is a Death Object?" a human asked.

"The stupidity of humans never ceases to amaze me. It is amazing you primitives can even begin to understand the grandeur of the universe," I said flicking my two tails harshly.

"Come, come now Tazzie. The humans are silly in their beliefs for sure but there is power in their ignorance. They are likely to be corrupted by the Death magic which this bowl serves as a container,"

"The question is what do the humans want us to help them with?" I asked staring at the tallest of the humans.

The humans grinned. "We need you to help us destroy it because it is making a madness spread over an entire world in the Republic,"

I gave Boss a sideways glance. It wasn't unheard of to hear about such an event happening, and I know there had been plenty of victims of Death Magic over the past tens of thousands of years.

But no humans or even Keres could touch a Death Object without falling under its corrupting power.

Boss held her hand over the surface of the bowl and bright white magic crackled in the air and I lent her some of my strength.

I could sense her magic trying to tap into the Darkness to study it, see what could happen and to see if there was a spirit we could fight.

But this was a unique Death Object that made the foul aroma of charred flesh, hair and death fill my senses.

"How did the humans touch this without fall to the Darkness?" I asked knowing it was impossible.

The humans looked nervously at each other. "We made a deal with a man that appeared when we touched the bowl,"

I prepared to pounce and Boss magicked a long purple sword out of thin air.

The humans grinned and they spoke as one. "It was a good deal for humanity. They sold their souls to me and in exchange I allow them to take the bowl off-world,"

Boss shook her head and I sensed her psychically battling with the Death creature that had clearly possessed the poor stupid humans.

The humans took a few steps back and I watched the humans and Boss stare into each other's eyes. There was clearly going to be as much a war of words here as much a psychic battle I was going to help with at some point.

"Why allow them to take the Bowl off-world?" Boss asked focusing on the humans intensely. "It makes no sense because you could corrupt millions of souls so why settle for three?"

"Because the humans would come here," I said staring at the bowl as the dark tendrils started to shrink back. Probably because the Death Creature had to use their magic in the mental battle with Boss instead of using it to protect the bowl.

That meant it was weaker.

Boss screamed out in pain and gripped her head as the Creature striked a mental blow.

I lent Boss all the strength I could.

Boss thrusted out her hand. Flattening a human against a wall. Bones cracked and organs exploded painting the walls of the office in dark red blood.

The other two humans laughed as their skin turned deathly black and their veins glowed sickly yellow.

The humans charged into each other and became one twisted, deformed walking corpse that made the air crackle with black magical energy.

"Death Creatures I hate them," I said my tails flickering around wildly.

I hissed as loud as I could sending the magical soundwaves slamming into the Creature.

Boss flew at the Creature. I had to do my part. I couldn't fight it. I still had to help Boss.

I spun around and focused on the evil Bowl. It was glowing dark evil black and I could sense the Darkness start to take root in the hull of the ship.

That had been the bastard's plan the entire time. Keres souls were brighter, purer and so-called tastier than human souls. So Geneitor planned to corrupt the ship inside out so he could force an entire ship's worth of Daughter of Genetrix to fall to his worship.

It was monstrous, pure monstrous.

I raised a paw. My claws shot out. I struck the Bowl.

Crippling pain filled me. My bones moved violently and I felt like my paw would shatter.

The Bowl hissed in pain as I realised how weak and helpless the Bowl was. It wasn't made from stone it was made from the dreams and delusions of the Death Creature.

It wasn't real. It was an abomination on the Goddess's work.

I clawed it again.

A massive chunk of it turned to ash but I was in agony. I was in so much crippling pain that I couldn't hiss or meow or do anything.

I tried to raise my claws again but I couldn't. I was in too much pain.

Boss screamed.

I spun around. Sending two fireballs at the Death Creature

allowing Boss to jump up and slash at his chest a little.

Pure magical energy filled me from the Goddess because I had to do this, I had to annihilate the bowl despite the pain but I couldn't.

But I had to do my duty.

I striked the bowl but my paw collapsed into the bowl like it had been eaten and all the pain receptors had been consumed.

I just looked down at my poor little paw as it was no longer there and I felt the corrupting influence of the Darkness pulse up my arm and my heartbeat flooded my body with the corrupted blood.

I felt the warmth and wonderful life that the Goddess filled me with start to become more distant as her power was fading from me.

Boss screamed as she realised I was dying and the Death Creature laughed.

I screamed in defiance and charged at the Bowl. The dark tendrils shot back in fear and I smashed into it with such force it flew off the desk.

Smashing onto the ground below. Turning to ash.

The Creature hissed and screamed out in a deafening roar as it started to dissolve because it couldn't remain in reality without an anchor. Something I had just annihilated.

As the threat was dead, the humans were no more and the ship was saved from Geneitor's corruption, I collapsed to the ground as my paws and body were slowly devoured by the corrupting Darkness that had taken root within me.

"At least Genetrix will grab my soul before Geneitor can torture it forever," I said trying to smile but accidentally flashing my fangs.

I could see how badly Boss wanted to touch me, cuddle me and stroke my blackening fur a final time. I would have loved that too but she couldn't become corrupted herself because the ship needed her, the Daughters of Genetrix needed her and most importantly the Goddess needed every able servant ready for the war to come.

Geneitor was growing stronger and stronger and if he reached full strength then he would happily devour all life in the galaxy and then the universe.

Something none of us could allow.

"I love you," I said to Boss. "You're a good woman, a good fighter and hell of a Servant of the Goddess,"

She smiled and I noticed a small crystal tear start to form in her eyes and she went to say something else.

But as the Darkness continued to dissolve my body and ears, I never heard the words but I knew they were words of thanks, appreciation and love. Because I might have been difficult at times but we were Familiar and Boss, a match made in the heavens and a bond that couldn't be broken because it was stronger than love and I really did love Boss.

And I was more than happy to have died to save her, the Keres and all the innocent people they would go on to save in the name of Genetrix, Goddess, Creator and Protector of life.

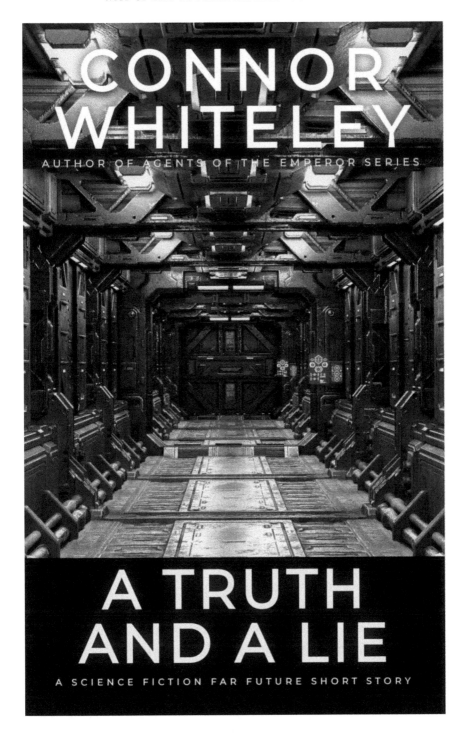

A TRUTH AND A LIE

If you asked any of the tens upon tens of trillions of humans in the Imperium how they would get access to forbidden knowledge, then there were only ever three answers. The most probable would be, they would simply report you to the authorities and you would never ever be seen again. The second answer would be you shouldn't because that is simply immoral and an affront to humanity and the Truth that the Rex lies about.

The third answer would be to find some kind of abomination like an alien, a historian or some kind of other forbidden creature that possessed such knowledge. The only problem with such things was that they were rarer than rare and you would most probably die in the process.

Thankfully that was not a problem for Commander Jerico Nelson.

Thick aromas of alcohol, sweat and wonderfully sweet chocolate filled Jerico's senses as he went inside The Lover's Bar onboard the disc-shaped space station known as Outpost-66.

Jerico smiled as he leant against the wonderfully warm grey metal doorway where a handful of people were coming and going. They were clearly military cadets judging by their cleanly pressed grey uniforms, and Jerico almost wanted to ask them where the hell they were off to.

It wasn't normal for any military units to be this far from civilisation, but he couldn't do that because he was hunted, keeping a low profile and he just couldn't draw attention to himself. And it wasn't like the military of the Imperium wasn't a massive Cult, if he spoke to the wrong person, then Earth would be told sooner or later.

Jerico shook his head at the very notion of Earth finding him.

Jerico hated how the entire bar was awful as a strategic position if anything went wrong.

The two rows of small metal tables pushed around the curved grey walls of the bar wouldn't provide any cover. But Jerico liked how people of all shapes, sizes and heights sat around the tables talking and laughing about their business. They were all drinking some kind of bright blue liquid that was probably strong enough to power small shuttles.

Jerico seriously didn't want to drink it if he could help it.

Jerico almost laughed as he saw three women in very attractive red dresses do some sort of exotic dancing on the oval platform in the middle of the bar. No one was paying attention to them so Jerico supposed their job was to simply get them in the bar.

But Jerico really didn't need them to get him in the bar.

Jerico went towards the massive bright red floating counter towards the very back of the bar. He clocked everyone was slowly looking at him, trying their best not to be seen, but he had been a Commander in the Imperial Army, he knew the signs of being watched. Jerico just needed to know how to find some forbidden information on a target and then he would leave all of these people in peace.

Most of them would hopefully be too drunk later on to remember him.

The closer he got to the counter the louder the humming, banging and popping of the space station got, it had faded as background noise so it was only now Jerico was realising the noise was still there. He still didn't like it, because it could easily hide the footsteps of enemies.

He gave the very tall woman behind the bar a friendly smile, but he was laughing more at himself than her. He just couldn't believe how obsessed he was with strategy and knowing how to win in a fight, he knew the skills were useful but they always popped up at weird times.

The woman smiled at Jerico as he leant against the icy coldness of the counter. The smells of oranges, lemons and grapefruits filled his senses making the great taste of lemon tarts form on his tongue.

"You want something that isn't alcohol, don't ya sweetheart?" the woman asked in a way that surprised Jerico. She sounded like she knew a lot more than Jerico wanted her to.

Jerico looked around the bar. All he wanted was a little information on where some human woman called Ithane Veilwalker could be, he had no idea what she really was. He was only going off what he had been told.

Jerico didn't believe for a single moment she was some woman who had been killed and brought back from the dead by some alien Goddess, but he had been gifted a task by a dying friend and he wanted to see it through.

"You seek someone," the woman said.

Jerico laughed and shook his head. He had no clue how to ask his question to this woman but he doubted she was as innocent or human as she appeared.

"I know if you want forbidden information then it is always best to start in the most remote regions of the Imperium," Jerico said keeping his voice as low as possible.

The woman smiled and nodded and Jerico looked around again and noticed a tall man wearing a black military uniform near the front door was watching them.

"Clearly I am not the only person who knows that little fact," Jerico said.

"Of course not," the woman said dropping her human-accent for just a moment.

Jerico took a step back and really looked at the woman. She looked so human with her thin waist, fat cheeks and long brown hair that she should be human.

But after a few moments, Jerico realised she was an alien Keres. He noticed how her ears might not have been pointed but they had been cut to remove the points, her waist was unnaturally thin and her facial features were all too perfect, too pointy, too human to be believable.

Jerico instantly wanted to reach for his pistol on his waist to protect her. Everyone in the Imperium knew to kill a Keres on site if they were found but Jerico couldn't allow that.

He had murdered way too many Keres over the decades out of blind obedience for him to let another human make the same mistakes he had.

Jerico leant very close to the Keres woman. "They will kill you if they find you,"

"I know," the woman said. "That is why the Man In Black is here. He had heard of magical miracles happening in this sector, I heal people you see who shouldn't be healed, so he came to investigate,"

"And now he wants to kill you," Jerico said hating the entire damn situation with the Imperium.

"If you help me escape then I promise you I will help you with whatever you need. Yet I need to know the topic,"

"I need to know where is Ithane Veilwalker?" Jerico asked, nodding.

The woman reached down below her counter and started to look like she was mixing drinks of some sort. Jerico really liked the intense aromas of orange and lemon and grapefruit but she was clearly acting.

The Man In Black was watching them intensely.

"Ithane Veilwalker is a myth created by your Imperium to give us false hope. The Keres are dying and we are being slaughtered by your Imperium. We want peace and you people enslave us,"

Jerico shook his head as he felt his necklace (that was apparently meant to contain the Soulstone of the Keres Goddess of Hope, Spero) pulse warmly around his neck.

Jerico took out the necklace and showed its bright blue jewel to the woman. "If that is a myth then why is Spero wanting me to find her?"

The woman's mouth dropped and Jerico could see she was conflicted and awed and even in a little fear as a drop of sweat rolled down her hand.

Then the woman laughed manically.

Jerico took a few steps back and whipped out his pistol.

The woman's veins turned black, black oil poured from her mouth and Jerico cursed under his breath. She was a Keres alright but she was a Dark Keres. She had sold her soul to the Keres God of Death Geneitor, a divine being devoted to the destruction of all life.

Or so the bullshit stories said.

Jerico aimed. He fired.

Bullets screamed through the air.

The woman laughed as she ate them and her arms transformed into immense black talons dripping dark red rich blood.

A scream came from behind.

Jerico spun around. He saw men and women run out of the bar screaming and shouting warnings as they went.

Space Station security would be there quickly. Jerico had to find his information soon.

The Black In Man charged at Jerico.

The woman flew forward.

Jerico rolled forward.

He fired at the Man.

The bullets bounced off him.

Jerico leapt up. The woman swung her talons at him.

Jerico blocked them. He punched her in the face.

Icy coldness shot up his arms.

The Man fired at the woman.

She screamed.

She shot out her arms. Black fire engulfed him.

He screamed in agony.

Jerico fired at the woman.

Tendrils of black fire melted the bullets but then the Man's screams just stopped and everything went silent.

When the silent flames finished crackling and engulfing the man, Jerico gasped as the Man was just a skeleton made from black crystal.

"Kill him," the woman said.

Jerico fired.

A bullet screamed towards the skeleton. It smashed into him. Shattering the crystal.

Jerico scanned the bar for the woman. She was gone.

He carefully searched behind the counter. He could sense her foul dark magic here. She was alive.

He just couldn't see her.

Jerico felt his heart pound in his chest. He felt sweat drip down his back. He could feel his fear responses kicking in.

Then Jerico's chest filled with the warmth of hope that Spero provided him with. He calmed down and he closed his eyes.

He wanted to sense the woman.

Air rushed behind him.

Jerico jumped forward. He opened his eyes.

He just missed two immense talons.

He fired into the air but he didn't hit anything.

Jerico closed his eyes again. He couldn't rely on human senses to find a Dark Keres. He had to rely on instinct.

Air zoomed towards him.

Jerico leapt to one side.

He felt the intense rush of heat flow past him. He wanted to panic at the idea of almost being cooked alive so he didn't allow himself to.

The air churned around him.

Jerico ducked. Fired three rounds all around him. He kicked the air.

He heard a scream as a bullet smashed into something and then his feet kicked the Keres's head.

Something cracked and Jerico opened his eyes to see the damn Keres woman collapse to the ground gripping her stomach as black blood poured out of the wound.

Jerico pointed his pistol firmly at her head but he was surprised that she was truly smiling at him. Her veins had returned to normal and Jerico had no idea how these Gods worked but he almost believed she had been freed of Geneitor's corrupting influence.

If such things actually happened.

"You helped me escape Geneitor. Thank you," the woman said weakly.

"Where is Ithane Veilwalker?" Jerico asked.

"The Father of Death knows. He tracks her but he only allows me to tell a lie and a truth before he claims my soul,"

"Speak and die then," Jerico said hating that he was being mean to a Keres that had probably only fallen to such corruption to survive humanity's onslaught.

"Ithane seeks the history of the Soulstones or Ithane can be found in the grave on Earth," the woman said before she died.

Jerico shook his head. It was clear that Ithane was alive, his old friend wouldn't have sent him on this mission if she could be found in a Grave so it was good to know he was looking for some History thing.

But Jerico just grinned to himself. His next task of following Ithane in her search for History was going to be next to impossible, everyone in the Imperium knew the Real History of everything was impossible to find.

The Rex had rewritten history thousands of thousands of times depending on what he wanted his human subjects to believe, so finding the True History of the Soulstones and anything related to the Keres was going to be next to impossible.

But as Jerico left the bar and looked for a shuttle to steal (ideally one that couldn't be traced), he was really excited for the future because this was going to be a hell of a mission and he truly loved impossible missions.

Especially when they involved hunting down impossible information and sorting fact from fiction in the crazy universe that was the Imperium.

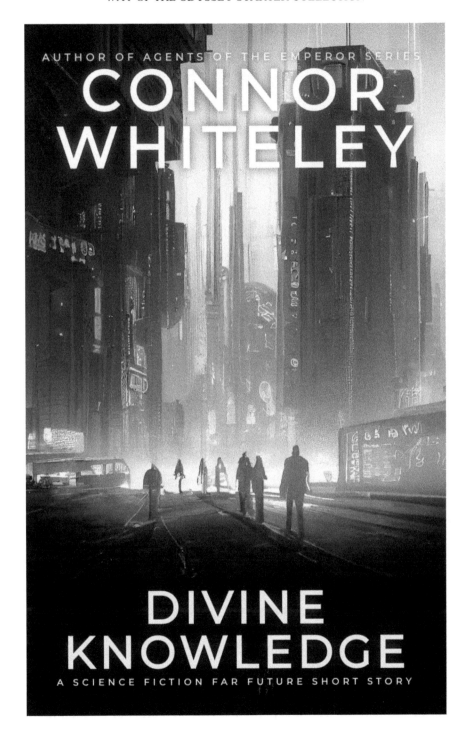

DIVINE KNOWLEDGE

"Impossible. The knowledge you seek is divine, forbidden and dangerous,"

Of all the sentences, Commander Jerico Nelson had suspected to hear as he sat down on a beautifully large golden throne-like chair, it certainly hadn't been that. He had wanted to come to the forbidden Enlightened Republic for the first time ever and he had wanted their help.

They were supposed to be the champions of Freedom, Democracy and everything the tyrannical Imperium wasn't, and yet they were still wanting to hide knowledge from him. Knowledge that might have been able to save everyone they loved and all of humanity.

Unless the Imperium finally launched an invasion of the Enlightened Republic and all of humanity killed each other in the process. Jerico seriously hoped that never ever happened, but it was only a matter of time.

Jerico just shook his head and he forced himself to look away from the ancient-looking elderly lady sitting at her oak desk in front of him. He liked how her long grey hair still looked full of life, joy and she was clearly healthy but she was just annoying him.

The entire chamber was actually rather good and Jerico really liked the beautiful yellow stone the high walls were made of. He wasn't too familiar with this particular type of stone but its shininess, strength and size certainly would have made it excellent cover to hide beneath in case of an attack.

Even the holo-art hanging on the yellow walls were impressive and Jerico was just happy he was here. The elderly woman might have been annoying, but this was the Enlightened Republic. It wasn't perfect but at least he could and probably would say whatever he wanted without getting arrested for simply disagreeing with the leadership.

"I will not give you any knowledge without permission," the elderly woman said as she stood up.

Jerico enjoyed the sweet aroma of roses, oranges and cloves that filled the air as she moved around, searching the immensely tall bookcase behind her.

Jerico watched her closely in case she was going to reach for a secret weapon or something. He seriously doubted she would but he couldn't be sure these days. He was already a former military Commander being hunted down in the Imperium for apparently betraying humanity.

He seriously couldn't believe the bullshit the Rex had spread about him. He wasn't a terrorist, a monster or a danger to the very fabric of the Imperium. Jerico had only realised decades too late that the alien Keres they were murdering were actually great, innocent people.

Humanity was only killing the Keres because humanity was scared of their innocent magic. Jerico hated the Rex and all the idiots that kept him in power.

"No," the woman said to herself as she searched through some of her books.

Jerico looked around and he was only going to give her a few more minutes before he forced the matter. He was searching for anything he could get his hands on about the so-called divine objects known as Soulstones.

He didn't believe in the Keres Gods or Goddesses at all (which even he admitted was odd considering he had been gifted a Keres necklace that was meant to be the Soulstone of the Keres Goddess of

Hope, Spero) and apparently the Soulstones contained the souls of the Gods and Goddesses of the Keres.

But he didn't buy it.

And as much as he wanted to just forget about these damn Soulstones, Jerico wasn't going to fail his old (dead) friend for a single moment. His friend had sent him on a mission to find some human woman that had been reborn by the Keres Goddess Genetrix and he was going to find her.

That search all rested on him finding out about the history of the Soulstones.

"I need that knowledge," Jerico said standing up, surprised as the taste of orange chicken formed on his tongue. It was one of the most amazing things Jerico had ever tasted.

"Do you like the taste?" the woman asked.

"What is this trick?" Jerico asked looking round for any food he might have missed. There wasn't any.

The woman laughed. "I am Knowledge Chief of the Republic. There isn't a single piece of history that flows through the Republic that gets past me,"

Jerico really enjoyed how the sensational taste of fruitiness orange and fresh chicken got more and more intense.

"So what is this orange chicken thing? Is this some kind of knowledge?" Jerico asked, not sure he wanted to know.

"Of course. There was a tribe about three thousand years ago that developed technology to manipulate the taste of their enemy's mouth to disarm them. It was very useful before the tribe killed them,"

"I am not your enemy,"

"I do not know that. In fact there has been a full squadron of Death Troopers watching and following you ever since you alerted us to your presence,"

Jerico paced around. "Surely that proves I am no threat to the Republic. And the Republic has spies in most corners of the Imperium, you must know they are hunting me as much as they can,"

"It could all be a deception and come on Commander, when has a Commander of the Imperium turn their back on the Rex?" the Knowledge Chief asked deadly serious.

Jerico laughed, not because it was funny, but because she was absolutely correct. Jerico had no idea if anyone in the history of humanity had ever betrayed the Rex. He personally handpicked each and every one of his Commanders and they had to be extremely brutal, murderous and some insane things to grab his attention.

Jerico hated himself for what he had done. He had burnt entire planets of Keres warriors before, or were they all warriors? Jerico knew those planets contained families, young people and so many innocents but he never questioned his orders.

Because what does the lives of some alien scum matter?

Jerico just looked at the Knowledge Chief. "How do I redeem myself? And how do I prove I am no threat to the Republic?"

The woman only grinned and Jerico couldn't help but get excited because this was going to be a very tough mission indeed.

***

Jerico flat out couldn't believe the sheer darkness of the long tunnel the Knowledge Chief was leading him down. He wasn't a massive fan of the immense yellow sandy blocks that made up the rough walls with bright almost blood-red cement filling the gap between each block.

Jerico wrapped his fingers round his pistol just in case this was some kind of trap, but as much as he didn't want to admit it, he just knew the Knowledge Chief wasn't going to kill him or trap him or do anything untoward.

He got the sense that she needed him for something, a task that no one had been willing or stupid enough to do.

Jerico kept following the Knowledge Chief down the tunnel, listening to his own awful breathing that he was trying and utterly failing to keep under control. The more he tried to focus and control his breathing the worse it got, and Jerico just focused on the Knowledge Chief.

He was almost surprised she was so confident, elegant and powerful considering how old she looked. Jerico didn't think she was wearing any technology or had any work done to her, but this was the Enlightened Republic. He wasn't too sure of the level of technology here, so anything was possible.

The wonderfully strange aroma of coffee, chocolate and strawberries filled Jerico's senses, making the delightful taste of strawberry shortcake form on his tongue, but then the Knowledge Chief stopped.

Jerico looked past her as a stupidly warm breeze brushed his cheeks and Jerico just knew that something wasn't natural about the tunnel.

Jerico looked at the Knowledge Chief who was grinning at him, almost like this was the last time she was ever going to see him. He was going to see her again no matter the cost and Jerico was going to survive this.

He hoped.

"What is this task then?" Jerico asked, not liking how the woman hadn't spoken to him for ages.

"This tunnel was originally created by the Keres when this world was owned by them. Then Geneitor unleashed a death curse on the world and there is a creature here that stirs," the Knowledge Chief said.

Jerico took out his pistol and shook his head.

"You might wonder why we haven't found the creature but the answer is simple. We have sent twenty men and women down here and none of them have returned. But I want to know what the Creature is and how to stop it from killing anyone else,"

Jerico nodded as he checked the sight on his pistol. "Actually my question was why build an entire human colony on a Keres Death World?"

The Knowledge Chief laughed. "Because only three people in the entire Republic know this is a Death World. Not even Supreme General Abbie knows this world's origin,"

Jerico wanted to argue with the Chief, because surely it was critical for the President of the Republic to know everything about her domain. But Jerico supposed that wasn't his problem, if the Republic relied on the same pack of lies, deception and falsehoods to remain as bound together as the Imperium. Then he didn't want to be here any longer than needed.

"I'll find the Creature for you but I am not killing it unless I have to," Jerico said not really knowing why he felt that way.

The Chief sighed and simply walked away.

Jerico went further down the hallway and enjoyed the wonderful warmth that flowed around him. He felt Spero's necklace pulse extra warmth into him and he knew this was a deception.

His footsteps echoed loudly in the hallway, a lot louder than they had a moment ago, and he could feel Spero trying to help him.

He still didn't believe in the stupid Keres Gods and Goddesses but whatever the magical thing in the necklace was, it wasn't trying to kill him. Which he seriously appreciated.

After walking down the hallway for a few minutes and the wonderfully intense aroma of chocolate, coffee and strawberry got even stronger, Jerico stopped as he felt like he was being watched.

He closed his eyes for a moment and then he opened them to see a man standing in front of him.

It was clearly a Keres man. His long pointy humanoid face was ghostly white, his ears were like daggers and his massive grin made Jerico uncomfortable. It was even worse that the man was unnaturally thin even by Keres standards and Jerico couldn't see any weapons.

That concerned Jerico a lot more than he ever wanted to admit.

Jerico blinked and he found himself standing in a hallway that was three times wider. It wasn't natural but nothing about Keres magic was. He couldn't allow himself to die.

"I am not an enemy," Jerico said with as much authority as he could.

The Keres man nodded and he started circling Jerico so Jerico did the same. When the Keres man took a step closer, Jerico took a step back and vice versa.

"I am aware of who and what and where you are, but who am not aware of why you are?" the Keres man asked.

Jerico shook his head. He hated some Keres, they were just flat out weird at times.

"I'm here to find out information about Ithane Veilwalker. Do you know her?" Jerico asked taking a few steps forward so the Keres took three steps back

"Of course. The Reborn, the Daughter of Genetrix, the Unpure Keres. Of course I know of her the entire galaxy sensed her Rebirth and everyone searches for her,"

Jerico wasn't sure he liked the idea of that. If this Ithane woman really was as important to the survival of all life in the galaxy, then Jerico hated to imagine what the Imperium would do to her if they found her. Let alone what the Dark Keres would do, the servants of the very Death God she was meant to obliterate.

The Keres man took four steps forward so Jerico did the same backwards.

"What do you know about her?" Jerico asked.

The warm air crackled with black magical energy. Jerico aimed his pistol at the Keres' head.

"Humans, always so focused on weapons and murder and death when I have the information you need. When Geneitor burnt this world and left me alive to warn others of similar sins he gifted me knowledge and power and magic,"

Jerico aimed his pistol right at the man's forehead. "I have seen the gifts that Geneitor spreads and it all ends with corruption and death. Tell me what you know and I might let you live,"

The Keres man laughed. "Live? Life? I am a servant of the God of Death. I do not care about life but now the Father of Death hunts you too. You have appeared in too many places not to be a threat,"

The Keres man screamed.

Jerico fired.

The Keres charged.
Bullets bounced off the Keres.
The Keres's arms became swords.
He swung at Jerico.
Jerico rolled backwards.
Jerico leapt up.
Firing his pistol until it was empty.
The Keres laughed.
The bullets screamed through the air.
Smashing into the Keres.
The bullets smashed onto the ground. They did nothing.
Jerico rolled his eyes. He hated this. He hated Dark Keres. Bullets were always useless.
The Keres leapt into the air.
Spinning around.
The air crackled with magical energy.
An invisible force gripped Jerico.
He tried to move. He couldn't.
His necklace glowed bright gold.
The Keres screamed in agony.
The force released him.
Jerico charged at the Keres.
Smashing his fists into the Keres.
The Keres hissed.
Jerico gripped the Keres's wrists.
Snapping it over his knee.
The Keres screamed in crippling pain.
Jerico whacked the Keres in the mouth.
The alien fell to the ground.
Jerico grabbed the alien by the neck and raised him over his head and smashed the Keres man over his knee. Shattering the Keres's spine.

An icy cold blast of air whipped past Jerico before he saw himself back in the same width of the hallway he had been in when the Knowledge Chief had left him, but the corpse of the Keres man was gone.

"He wouldn't have killed too many more people you know," a man said behind him.

Jerico looked behind him and frowned as he saw a floating skull. "What the hell are you?"

The skull laughed. "I must keep this short because I cannot control things in your reality for too long. But that Creature only would have kept killing humans whenever a human was stupid enough to enter the tunnels,"

"But the Chief Knowledge mentioned in passing these tunnels were sealed," Jerico said.

"Young adults, young couples and even the adventurous old always find a way into restricted tunnels so he killed them and fed me the souls," the skull said rotating to the left.

Jerico took a few steps back as he realised he was speaking to some sort of strange version of Geneitor, or at least that was what this skull wanted him to believe.

"You aren't Geneitor so go," Jerico said aiming his empty pistol at the skull and just hoping the skull didn't realise how empty the threat was.

The skull laughed. "And so my wife places the fate of the galaxy in a human woman and a man that doesn't believe in the Divine battle he is walking into. Oh this will be fun my love. Let the Games begin,"

Jerico was about to punch the skull when it fell to the ground and turned to dust.

Jerico couldn't help but feel like he was entering a war on a scale he couldn't even begin to imagine.

And he wasn't sure if that scared or excited him a lot more than he ever wanted to admit.

***

A few hours later, Jerico leant on the massive oak desk in the Chief Knowledge's office as she just sat there looking, smiling and humming at him. She still looked as ancient as she did earlier but Jerico had to admit she looked good knowing he was alive and successful on his mission.

Her hair was still full of life, joy and looked healthy so clearly life in the Republic wasn't so bad even if the city and colony were built on a Keres Death World. Something Jerico fully intended to share with someone at some point.

"Do you have my information?" Jerico asked. "I need access to the Soulstones records,"

The Knowledge Chief laughed. "We don't have any records pertaining to such forbidden knowledge,"

Jerico slammed his fists on the desk. He hated this stalling, he hated the Republic, he hated how everyone was trying to stop him on his mission.

"Because the records never existed in the first place at least not in a manner that humans could understand," the Chief Knowledge said.

Jerico looked around the entire damn office in frustration, hoping that there was a book or something he could grab or steal just so he could find some answers. But the entire silly chamber was just as good as it looked earlier with its beautiful yellow stone walls and impressive holo-art.

She really was telling the truth.

Jerico wanted to argue but he knew, just knew she was telling the truth. There probably were records available in the galaxy about the Soulstones but they were probably written in Keres or ancient Keres.

Something none of them could understand and even though the Republic protected the Keres as much as they could, Jerico doubted the Keres would be too willing to share such knowledge with them. Especially with the constant threat of Imperial spies.

"But," the Knowledge Chief said, "if I have learnt one thing in my long life about the Keres, it is that their magic runs on emotion and it is that emotion that will lead you to your goal,"

Jerico went to laugh but he hissed in pleasure as Spero pulsed loving warmth into his heart. And Jerico realised that he had a good idea where to find the Soulstones or at least find Ithane Veilwalker.

If he was a Keres God or Goddess (creatures that didn't really exist) then Jerico supposed he would feel safe on the world famous for where they apparently walked.

"Genesis," Jerico said. "The so-called Mother World of the Keres, the world where the Gods and Goddesses first walked on Holy ground,"

Jerico was rather impressed that he actually knew that, but he was fairly sure Spero had implanted some of the information in his head.

"And it is said that where their bare feet touched the ground ten thousand gemstones reaching to the planet's very core was planted," the Chief Knowledge said grinning like a schoolgirl.

"Bullshit, surely?" Jerico asked.

The Chief Knowledge laughed. "The Mother of Life has destined you for greatness but it will be a journey that will test you for sure. Now go dear Traveler because you will not be the only person to make this connection, darker forces now turn their gaze to the Mother World,"

"And soon another battle will be fought," Jerico said knowing exactly the sort of rubbish so-called mythic people tried to place.

Jerico nodded his thanks to the woman and as he went out of the chamber he felt pure excitement fill him because he was almost at the end of his journey. Once he found Ithane Veilwalker and made sure she was okay, he would have done his dead friend proud and he could go back to his old life of being hired protection and he wouldn't have to deal with anything more about the Keres, their Gods and their magic.

But he couldn't deny the chance of that was slim to none and that made him more excited than any guy had any right to feel.

AUTHOR OF AGENTS OF THE EMPEROR SERIES

CONNOR WHITELEY

IN DEFENCE OF FREEDOM

A SCIENCE FICTION SPACE OPERA SHORT STORY

IN DEFENCE OF FREEDOM

This was the hour I died.

You see when I was a child, maybe two or three years old, my mother and father sacrificed their lives to smuggle me from the dark tyranny of the Imperium to a place called the Enlightened Republic. I never knew my mother or father, not really anyway, I sometimes have weird images appear in my head of them smiling, kissing my head and the three of us just laughing together.

I knew they really, really loved me.

So as I stood in the brand-new clinically white spherical bridge of my white circular warship, The Hammer of Freedom, I was really hopeful they would be proud of me because I was helping to defend the place they died trying to get me to.

The bridge I had to admit was strange to be in after training for so long. I had always loved the smooth angelic designs of the bridge with its curved walls, bright white walls and flooring that helped to make the bridge feel like daytime even though we were in space and I did like the metal grey throne that I could sit on.

I never did sit on it really. My command throne was just so icy cold and whenever I did sit on it, it just made the situation too real and it reminded me that too many lives depended on my actions.

If I ever failed in my duties to the Enlightened Republic then so many billions of lives were as good as dead. That was a hell of a burden to carry around.

Even the wonderful taste of creamy apple pie clinging to the air wasn't enough to relax me because I knew an attack could happen at any moment. But that apple pie with hints of caramel, ice cream and sweet bitter apples was just sensational.

There were twenty other men and women in the bridge with me and they were all as amazing as each other. I know the whole myth around captain-don't-have-favourites but right now it truly isn't a myth. I loved them all.

My first mate Piper was standing closest to me as she finished running a scan of the nearby area and she was analysing the results like they were the difference between life and death.

Maybe they were.

The entire crew was doing something and I admired that. I had served on warships before and I seriously hated how some crews were lazy when at any moment the Imperium could attack to enslave us.

I had lost way too many friends like that, but at least my crew weren't like that.

They were all so helpful, kind and supportive as they walked around the bridge in their clinically white uniform with a golden pin badge of an angel over their chest symbolising how the Republic was always about freedom, choice and justice.

Nothing like the evil Imperium was. That was all about control, death and murder. The Imperium and their cold leader the Rex were some of the most monstrous people I had ever met.

At least I was safe here away from the evil Imperium as the warship just floated peacefully in space waiting for danger to find us. There weren't any planets nearby, the stars were cold and distant and I couldn't help but wonder why this position needed to be defended.

But apparently according to Supreme General Abbie, this was one of the most important positions to defend in the entire Republic. And I always did what she told me.

"Enemy contacts incoming," Piper said way too calmly for my liking.

"Report," I said, really wanting this to be a joke.

Piper tapped on the massive floor-to-ceiling windows that covered two sides of the bridge and it zoomed in on three incoming circular warships sending out Imperial signals.

"Prepare for battle but don't fire until I give the command," I said.

Everyone nodded and Piper relayed the orders to the rest of my fleet, another three warships, and my heart leapt to my chest.

The Imperial warships were shiny, brand-new and there wasn't even a single dent in the cold black exterior of the incoming balls of death.

They probably had the best weapons and I knew if they got past us then they could easily jump into Ultraspace and attack the heart of the Republic.

As much as I hated the Ultraspace tunnel network at times because every so often you needed to enter three or four different tunnel networks to get to your destination. Sometimes the Ultraspace network was the only thing protecting the Republic.

Otherwise it would be way too easy for the Imperium to launch their battlefleet into the heart of the Republic and enslave millions.

"Captain, they're haloing us," Piper said.

I looked at her smooth beautiful face and nodded so she would put them through.

No visuals came up but all I was heard the damp heavy breathing of a man before he started talking.

"Captain Thomas Crane you are a good man and we need your help getting into the Republic. We are refugees seeking protection against the Imperium and you need to let us through," the man said.

"Considering I can't even see you that's a firm no. I like to see who I'm talking to," I said knowing this had to be a trap.

The man laughed and Piper took a step closer to me as did a tall man called Bob that I hadn't had a chance to talk to too much.

A moment later a very overweight man appeared in holographic form on the window and I smiled at him knowing that my background was blurred.

"I know you are not a refugee ship," I said. "Your weapons are too new, your ships are too good and you are fools for thinking the Republic would allow such threats into their space,"

The man cocked his head. "I thought the Republic were welcoming,"

"We welcome everyone trying to escape the Imperium but I do not welcome brand-new warships with powerful weapons into our space,"

My bridge went silent and other crew members came closer to me as others stepped away to do their job.

The overweight man grinned at me. "I did tell the Rex this was a stupid idea so I will be frank. My ship is armed with nuclear warheads as are the two warships next to me that are filled with over ten million people wanting to get into the Republic,"

My stomach twisted.

"We collected these people as they tried to flee so the deal is you let me and my forces into the Republic or we kill ten million people. Their blood will be on your hands. I'll give you one minute to decide. If you don't pick up they die,"

Before I could say anything the idiot hung up and I just looked at my crew as they frowned at me. Their eyes were wide and I was almost disappointed that they didn't look like they had any ideas.

I shook my head at them. "It's an impossible choice. If we don't allow them into the Republic then the innocent people die. If you allow them into the Republic then they could kill tens upon tens of millions,"

"It should be a logical choice," Piper said.

"Then why does it feel so hard?" I asked.

My entire crew looked at me and weakly smiled. "Because you're a good man,"

I wasn't so sure about that, I did some questionable things in the Republic Army a few years ago but I got the point.

"What do you need from us?" they asked.

And all I knew was that I absolutely had to try and save these ten million people that were perfectly innocent onboard those warships.

I had to protect the Republic, save the people and protect my crew at the same time. Surely it couldn't be that hard.

"Those nukes onboard the warships, they would have to be detonated remotely right?" I asked.

A young man called Frank came up to the front of the crew and smiled at me. He was a great engineer from what the others had said, it was just a shame this was the first time we were talking.

"Correct sir. Imperial Protocol is to only allow the lead vessel access to the nukes,"

"He's calling again," Piper said.

I nodded and a moment later the fat overweight man reappeared.

"I presume you won't want to save these ten million people but when me and my father went out hunting for scummy poor people when I was a kid. I used to get great joy out of watching the poor scumbags trying to escape my traps. I'll be watching and please, give me a good show before I kill you all,"

He cut the line and I did a quick scan to make sure he wasn't watching us by hacking into our systems. He hadn't thankfully.

"We need to call for reinforcements," a woman said.

I shook my head. "Negative, we need to find a solution. Carry on Frank,"

Frank nodded. "The nukes can only be controlled *and* deactivated from the lead vessel but everything operates on a very sophisticated signal,"

I pointed to the three Imperial warships. "Can you hack into that signal setup and deactivate the nukes from here?"

Frank came to stand next to me and folded his arms. "Negative. I know Republic tech is based on Imperial ones but we use completely different tech setups and I'm not skilled enough to work out the differences,"

I nodded. It was annoying but I understood. I just wanted to protect those innocent people. Then I realised there might have been another way.

I was about to ask about contacting Frank's old boss to see if she could talk him through it but I hated what Piper said next.

"Enemy forces incoming," Piper said.

I double-tapped the window and the ship's computer systems zoomed in the Imperial vessels. They were heading full steam towards us within five minutes they would be within firing range.

We all had to come up with a solution right now.

"I need to do something," I said trying to remember anything at all about my training or records or similar accounts that I've read over the decades.

Nothing. I didn't have a clue.

Then I wondered what if I made an impossible bargain that would kill me but save everything I loved.

I looked at Frank. "Could you give me a device that would scan a ship's signals and hijack any nuke-relate ones?"

Frank nodded. "I can do that. You would be closer to the source so it would be easier than doing it remotely. Why?"

I just looked at the incoming enemy warships and smiled. "Because I'm going on board that warship, I'm going to die and I'm going to save everyone,"

My entire crew shook their heads and the deadly silence told me everything I needed to know.

We all knew it was the only way.

***

I was somewhat surprised how easy it was to get the Imperial commander to allow me to go onto the bridge, they didn't even search me because apparently the Republic was so pathetic it wasn't a threat, but now my stomach was twisting into an agonising knot as I realised what was going to happen next.

I stood in the middle of a large boxroom of a bridge with awful cream-coloured walls, a horrible smell of bleach and the overweight male commander just stunk of tobacco.

Unlike before on the hologram I could now see the commander

was ugly with blackened teeth, an immense beer gut that came from drinking too much instead of doing your duty and his black hair looked like a bird's nest more than anything else.

I was the only other person on the bridge besides the commander and I so badly wanted to kill him as he wore his ugly black Imperial Army uniform, but instead I just smiled and I pressed the button on a small black device that started searching for nuke signals.

The realisation was finally hitting me that I was going to die. I didn't want to die, I hated dying, I almost felt like I was betraying the sacrifice of my parents. But all I wanted, needed to do with my life was protect the Republic, the innocent and my crew.

If dying meant doing that then I was happy to do it.

"What's the plan now then?" the Commander asked.

"There isn't one or to be honest, I'm hoping you'll be talking long enough for me to escape and kill you," I said lying.

The Commander nodded like he believed me but then he frowned as a red light on his wrist started flashing.

"Lying to me isn't good. I know you're searching for nuclear signals and, what? You wanted to hijack the signals and deactivate them?"

I didn't dare react. He could have been fishing and I was not going to confirm his crazy ideas about me.

"Shame," he said, "I was hoping for a good show but you see the nukes aren't all tied together and I don't control them,"

I just looked at him.

"This is a suicide mission for both of us it seems," the commander said. "The Rex controls the nukes and I failed him too many times so now he wants to kill me, your Republic and the refugees in the two other ships,"

I didn't want to believe this but from everything I've heard from others fleeing the Imperium, the historical documents I'd read and the things I saw when I visited the Imperium twice, I knew he was telling the truth. The Rex really was that crazy.

"I'm sorry," the commander said. "I'm sorry for all of this and now I don't know how to fix this,"

A loud deafening roar echoed overhead and I presumed that was the sound of the nukes charging up. They were going to explode shortly.

I had to find a way out of this. I had to live. I had to save the innocent people.

"We have to save them," I said. "Don't you Imperial guys have signal blockers?"

The commander shrugged and just stared into space like it was the last thing he might ever see. It probably would be unless he helped me.

But he was useless.

I hadn't focused on the walls or equipment in the boxroom bridge before so I went over to some kind of cuboid thing and pressed some of the switches on it.

A whole bunch of communication channels started to appear, I looked through the call history and found my ship. I dialled.

A moment later Piper's wonderful face appeared.

"Get me Frank now," I said.

Frank's face appeared.

"I need to know how to block signals,"

Frank nodded. "Okay you need to enter the following code very carefully into the Imperial vessel. My old mentor taught me this as a joke and-"

"Don't have time for this," I said.

Then Frank told me exactly what to do about the code. The deafening scream of the nuclear warheads got louder and louder and I typed faster and faster.

I entered the code and then the nukes started popping.

Then silence.

The communication channel with Frank cut out and the commander just looked at me and grinned.

Then he pulled a gun out.

"Thanks for saving me mate," he said. "But I cannot let you live. There is still hope for me with the Rex. You might have blocked the signals he was sending but I can prove myself useful,"

As he kept preaching his pathetic delusions about how the Rex might forgive him (but if the Rex was prepared to nuke him I doubt it) I accessed the signals and computer systems that kept the nukes linked together and a simple diagram appeared.

The diagram showed how I could deactivate the two nukes on the other warships if I wanted to and I could activate any of the nukes I wanted.

So I disconnected the two ships with the innocent people onboard and I just looked at the commander who was still being pathetic.

"And then the Rex will have no choice than to accept me," he said.

"You're mad," I said.

The commander stormed over to me and pressed the gun into my mouth and I just smiled.

As I pressed the nuclear-arming button, I watched as the two innocent warships flew off to one side out of danger and I let the sheer deafening roar of the warning alarms echo around the bridge.

My ears started to bleed but I didn't care because I had done my mission.

My mission was to always protect the Republic, protect my crew and save innocent people fleeing from the Imperium. My mum and dad had sacrificed their lives for me to do that and now I was sacrificing my life to save others.

I laughed as my life really was perfect and this was a great full-circle moment and as the panic reached the commander's eyes, I almost felt sorry for him.

He could have lived. We all could have lived but it was his delusions that made me do this.

As the nukes went off ripping the ship into thousands of shards and ripped my body to shreds I just grinned and hoped that my parents would be proud of me and I could finally be reunited with them.

Just like I had always wanted.

WAY OF THE ODYSSEY STARTER COLLECTION

SOCIALLY CRIMINAL

Justice Aisha Roar sat on her favourite cold, damp and sticky wooden bar stool in the messy Public House just off Main Street in the heart of the criminal underworld. The light was dark, scary and criminally good just how she liked it and the pub was thankfully filled with her favourite people tonight.

She sat towards the back like she always did and she pressed her black-armoured back against the sticky wooden walls that stunk of cheap alcohol, sex and sweat, just like how a good pub should smell. There were a few floating orbs of light swimming around against the dirty black ceiling providing just enough light, but it wasn't like anyone here actually wanted to see anyone's faces.

Everyone here was just here to drink, be merry and maybe have some random sex because it just felt good in the moment.

Aisha had always loved her time here and the constant background noise of people talking, laughing and shouting made her thinly smile. It was always great to be here after a long day of hunting down criminals and killing them because that was the law, but she always loved a good drink even more.

There was a brand-new wooden stage up at the front of the pub which Aisha really didn't like, because there was some hip-pop rubbish band from Earth playing there.

Aisha really didn't know what crime those fools had committed to end up in some junk bar like this one. The musicians were good, damn good so Aisha just couldn't understand whatsoever why these people wanted to play here.

They could easily get thousands of Rexes and then even more through tips if they played in the Spires, where the posh people lived. So maybe their crime was just stupidity and Aisha was half tempted to donate some of her money to them but she had already met her personal monthly quota of charity giving.

And she wouldn't want to get a foul reputation as a do-gooder. She actually shuddered at the very idea.

A cute young couple walked past her table, the woman looked okay wearing a very short black skirt, and the young man looked stunning in his tight jeans, shirt and boots. Hopefully both of them were in for a lucky night tonight, but Aisha was still alone.

Most of the Justices on the planet preferred to be alone because it was what their job required, each Justice was a law onto themselves and no one except the Glorious Rex himself on Earth could ever challenge their judgement.

It didn't make dating easy, it certainly made having a family impossible but Aisha still loved her job. It was her small way of helping to make the Imperium a better place with less freaks, criminals and alien scum in it.

"Lady Justice," a man said coming over to the table.

Aisha rolled her eyes. As much as she loved helping people, donating secretly to charities and making the Imperium a safer place, everyone knew never to disturb a Justice when they were drinking.

There might not have been a lot of social activity in the Imperium outside of work, watching fights and gambling, but drinking was a sacred activity of the Justices.

"I was hoping to have a moment of your time in exchange for this," the man said.

A small floating orb of light hovered over head and Aisha had a feeling that the owner of the pub was watching her, technically illegally but privacy was a joke these days.

Aisha focused on the small crystal glass of golden liquid and she instantly knew it was a very fine whiskey not found on this planet.

That had to have cost the man a few thousand Rexes, so why was he giving it to her?

Aisha looked at the man and he was surprisingly young with smooth sexy features, a pretty face and his slim body looked amazing in his tight robes denoting he was from the local College.

Definitely a man that did not belong in the deepest, darkest depths of this planet.

"Are there not Justices at the Colleges? In the Spires? In your own family?" Aisha asked.

The floating orb of light dipped a little lower and if it dared to get much closer then Aisha would happily smash it. What could the owner of the pub do? Call the Justices?

"Of course but I require a more roguish touch for my problem and I know you have a very effective reputation for getting rid of people," the man said.

Aisha had to admit she loved how her reputation was finally taking shape but she really didn't want this young man thinking that Justices were dangerous, it was the criminals they hunted that they were the real danger. Then she just smiled because the constant indoctrination that all subjects of the Imperium went through should take care of that.

"Of course, if your target has committed a crime then they will die. That is the law. If they steal a slice of bread, they die. If they assault someone, they die. If they murder someone, they die," Aisha said.

The young man frowned a little. "My wedding application got denied recently and I want you to fix it,"

Aisha smiled. It was a great effective feature of the Imperium that in order for two people to get married the Rex had to personally approve it and even then they could only get married if it served the Imperium.

A lot of maths, statistics and problem-solving was used to calculate how great the marriage would impact the Imperium and most of the time marriages were accepted. It was important to the fabric of society that the rich only married the rich, doctors only married doctors and the poor only married the poor. It was critical to stop the corrupting influence of the lower classes from ruining the rich people that were actually going to make something of themselves.

Aisha wasn't always sure she agreed with but it was an interesting idea.

"The Rex made his decision, even a Justice cannot overrule them. What were the stated reasons?" Aisha asked.

"I cannot marry my girlfriend because I am a student and she is a military Commander two years older than me,"

Aisha nodded. That was strange and it meant that the girlfriend had to come from a military family to get promoted that quickly. But students and military types were always marrying.

Except when one thing was revealed.

"What are you studying in?" Aisha asked.

The man smiled and Aisha smiled too. He was clearly passionate about it, so it had to be something grand like the military, sciences, medicine or a whole host of other brilliant subjects.

"I'm studying game design," the man said.

Aisha just reached across the table, grabbed the man's whiskey and downed it in one.

There was nothing kind she could say to the man because game design was useless to helping the Imperium survived so he was a useless man. But it was clear as day that he loved the subject.

And Aisha had always respected passion.

"And I refused to take the propaganda module," the man said.

Out of instinct Aisha moved her hand down to her waist where her gun was but she stopped her. This young man wasn't a radical that was a danger to the Imperium. He was just a young man that wanted to marry his girlfriend.

He did not need to die no matter how many of her peers would have killed him for not helping the Imperium indoctrinate young minds through games.

That was actually a crime so technically she had to kill this young man but she wanted to learn more and help him.

And if she found more evidence of his crimes against the Imperium then she would sadly have to kill him.

"I've come to you because the personal reference on my marriage application lied about me," the man said.

Aisha leant forward. Now that was a much more serious crime.

"What's your name?" Aisha asked as she stood up and downed the rest of her drink in one.

"Joshua Laurie," he said.

Aisha grabbed him and took him out of the pub. "Well Joshua, take me to this liar and then we will see how he committed the most outrageous crime imaginable. They lied to the Glorious Rex himself,"

Aisha felt so excited as they left the pub because she was finally going to hunt down her criminal.

A criminal that might need the ultimate punishment.

***

Aisha was hardly surprised too much when Joshua led her down through the dirty, stinky and toxic narrow streets of the criminal underworld with her fingers tightly on the trigger of her gun.

Then Joshua led her into a very crawl and dirty metal chamber inside an abandoned building. The chamber itself was immense covered with black mouldy walls, puddles of stagnant water covered the floor as did streaks of brown dried blood.

Aisha just smiled as she watched two very attractive middle-aged men clearing up after the fight that had caused the streaks of blood, and judging by the sheer amount of holo-cigars, bullets and broken weapons there must have been a hell of a crowd here tonight.

There were only three social activities in all of the Imperium. There was drinking which Aisha loved, there was watching or taking part in fights or there was gambling. Aisha really didn't like the last two because she preferred fighting on the streets (illegal to all but Justices) and gambling was just stupid.

But judging by the chamber some people seriously loved

watching a good fight.

"This is the man that lied on my application," Joshua said pointing to one of the two middle-aged men.

Aisha pointed her gun at him and just focused on how disgusting he looked in his dirty cloak, soaked-through boots and blackened teeth.

"Why the hell did you want this man on your wedding application?" Aisha asked.

"Because I'm his father," the man said.

Aisha just shook her head. There really was no ending to humanity's stupidity and it made no sense how this man working in the criminal underworld had managed to get a son into a local College. That should have been impossible.

Aisha made a note to herself to investigate the College tomorrow. There was no telling if Joshua's criminal family might have started corrupting the rich students of the College.

"Why did you lie dad on my application? I saw it and you said I was unfaithful to my girlfriend and I had donated to pro-Keres charities,"

Aisha pointed the gun at the son. The Keres were foul alien abominations that wanted to destroy humanity and their way of life. It was an awful crime to help them.

"Relax Lady Justice, he did no such thing," the father said.

Aisha decided to put her gun away because these two people made no sense and their actions literally went against how the Imperium worked.

"How are you two even related? There are strict laws against poor degenerates going to College. How did you get in?" Aisha asked.

Joshua smiled. "My girlfriend pulled a few strings and got me into college. I rose up through the class quickly and effectively and now I'm on the Student Council,"

As much as Aisha wanted to be annoyed that a poor person had a position of power in the local College, she actually couldn't be annoyed. The man was clearly intelligent, kind and passionate and of course Aisha would never admit this to her peers but the Imperium needed more people like that.

And so many of the laws were just dumb social laws to control others that it was just so stupid.

Poor people needed to go to College, get educated and help the Imperium, because the rich people were hardly doing an amazing job.

The father came over to Aisha. "Please don't arrest me and my son. We're good people, I provide innocent workers with sanctioned entertainment and that is what my son wants to do. We want to be entertainers, not criminals,"

All of Aisha's instincts, training and textbooks were telling her to just kill these two people now because they were a theoretical threat to the Imperium, but they weren't.

They seriously weren't.

Aisha knew that the father just wanted to entertain people as did the son just through different methods, but there was still one important question left.

"Why didn't you want your son getting married?" Aisha asked.

The father looked at the ground focusing on a long streak of blood that looked impossible to clean.

"I wanted my son to marry who he actually loves. He doesn't love the military girl, they both only wanted sex from each other and they were both using each other,"

Aisha looked at Joshua. "Is this true?"

Joshua nodded like he was proud of it. "Yeah. She wanted to have sex with a poor degenerate for the thrill and I wanted to go to College. I wanted her as much as she wanted me but when her father started asking questions she wanted to get married to protect herself,"

"And you didn't?" Aisha asked.

Joshua nodded and Aisha had to admit it was nice when the father hugged his son, that was a rare sight these days in the Imperium. A very unfortunate day.

As Aisha just looked at the father and son she couldn't deny how badly the law said they both had to die. The father had lied to the Rex himself, the son had illegally gone to College and used a military girl for his own gain (a strange little law made that illegal) and even the girlfriend needed to die technically because she had been having sex outside her permissible social rank.

It was all so stupid and as much as it would end Aisha's life, career and drinking fund if anyone found out she simply lowered her gun and walked away.

There were no crimes here, not real ones anyway, and all these social crimes were all victimless but Aisha still had to investigate the College just in case.

But she really, really hoped that Joshua would find happiness because it was the very least that everyone deserved.

***

Aisha had loved stalking the long perfectly clean, refreshingly nutty-scented air of the local College as she had investigated for any sign of corruption amongst the local rich students, and thankfully there had been none. In fact they seemed to be even more dedicated and indoctrinated into the Imperial Cult that worshipped everything the Rex said as divine law.

That was brilliant for the sake of the Imperium.

As Aisha sat later that night at the back of the bar again resting her black armour against the wooden sticky walls and her hands wrapped around a wonderfully cold tankard of beer, she was really happy with herself.

Because by proving that the law was wrong about the strict social controls of the Imperium, maybe she could get them to be dropped as laws and then the Rex's plans for mass indoctrination could be even stronger, better and more effective so no one could ever question the righteousness of his rule.

Then maybe there would be less criminals and that meant more drinking time in this great pub. Aisha really did enjoy the constant sweet aromas of sweat, stale beer and sex, there was just nothing else like it.

And in a cold, unloving galaxy, Aisha knew that love was always needed and now Joshua was alive and free to find who he loved and hopefully Aisha could find someone to love her in the end.

She smiled at that, that really would be an amazing thing to have.

But until then would always be more criminals, more murders and thieves to find, investigate and kill and that seriously excited Aisha a lot more than she ever wanted to admit.

WAY OF THE ODYSSEY STARTER COLLECTION

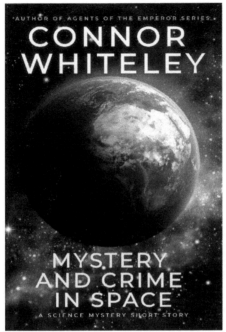

GET YOUR FREE SHORT STORY NOW! And get signed up to Connor Whiteley's newsletter to hear about new gripping books, offers and exciting projects. (You'll never be sent spam)
https://www.subscribepage.io/garrosignup

About the author:

Connor Whiteley is the author of over 60 books in the sci-fi fantasy, nonfiction psychology and books for writer's genre and he is a Human Branding Speaker and Consultant.

He is a passionate warhammer 40,000 reader, psychology student and author.

Who narrates his own audiobooks and he hosts The Psychology World Podcast.

All whilst studying Psychology at the University of Kent, England.

Also, he was a former Explorer Scout where he gave a speech to the Maltese President in August 2018 and he attended Prince Charles' 70th Birthday Party at Buckingham Palace in May 2018.

Plus, he is a self-confessed coffee lover!

Other books by Connor Whiteley:
Bettie English Private Eye Series
A Very Private Woman
The Russian Case
A Very Urgent Matter
A Case Most Personal
Trains, Scots and Private Eyes
The Federation Protects
Cops, Robbers and Private Eyes
Just Ask Bettie English
An Inheritance To Die For
The Death of Graham Adams
Bearing Witness
The Twelve
The Wrong Body
The Assassination Of Bettie English
Wining And Dying
Eight Hours
Uniformed Cabal
A Case Most Christmas

Gay Romance Novellas
Breaking, Nursing, Repairing A Broken Heart
Jacob And Daniel
Fallen For A Lie
Spying And Weddings
Clean Break
Awakening Love
Meeting A Country Man
Loving Prime Minister
Snowed In Love
Never Been Kissed

Love Betrays You

Lord of War Origin Trilogy:
Not Scared Of The Dark
Madness
Burn Them All

Way Of The Odyssey
Odyssey of Rebirth
Convergence of Odysseys

The Fireheart Fantasy Series
Heart of Fire
Heart of Lies
Heart of Prophecy
Heart of Bones
Heart of Fate

City of Assassins (Urban Fantasy)
City of Death
City of Martyrs
City of Pleasure
City of Power

Agents of The Emperor
Return of The Ancient Ones
Vigilance
Angels of Fire
Kingmaker
The Eight
The Lost Generation
Hunt

Emperor's Council
Speaker of Treachery
Birth Of The Empire
Terraforma
Spaceguard

The Rising Augusta Fantasy Adventure Series
Rise To Power
Rising Walls
Rising Force
Rising Realm

Lord Of War Trilogy (Agents of The Emperor)
Not Scared Of The Dark
Madness
Burn It All Down

Miscellaneous:
RETURN
FREEDOM
SALVATION
Reflection of Mount Flame
The Masked One
The Great Deer
English Independence

OTHER SHORT STORIES BY CONNOR WHITELEY

Mystery Short Story Collections

Criminally Good Stories Volume 1: 20 Detective Mystery Short Stories

Criminally Good Stories Volume 2: 20 Private Investigator Short Stories

Criminally Good Stories Volume 3: 20 Crime Fiction Short Stories

Criminally Good Stories Volume 4: 20 Science Fiction and Fantasy Mystery Short Stories

Criminally Good Stories Volume 5: 20 Romantic Suspense Short Stories

Connor Whiteley Starter Collections:
Agents of The Emperor Starter Collection
Bettie English Starter Collection
Matilda Plum Starter Collection
Gay Romance Starter Collection
Way Of The Odyssey Starter Collection
Kendra Detective Fiction Starter Collection

Mystery Short Stories:
Protecting The Woman She Hated
Finding A Royal Friend
Our Woman In Paris
Corrupt Driving
A Prime Assassination
Jubilee Thief
Jubilee, Terror, Celebrations
Negative Jubilation
Ghostly Jubilation
Killing For Womenkind

WAY OF THE ODYSSEY STARTER COLLECTION

A Snowy Death
Miracle Of Death
A Spy In Rome
The 12:30 To St Pancreas
A Country In Trouble
A Smokey Way To Go
A Spicy Way To GO
A Marketing Way To Go
A Missing Way To Go
A Showering Way To Go
Poison In The Candy Cane
Kendra Detective Mystery Collection Volume 1
Kendra Detective Mystery Collection Volume 2
Mystery Short Story Collection Volume 1
Mystery Short Story Collection Volume 2
Criminal Performance
Candy Detectives
Key To Birth In The Past

Science Fiction Short Stories:
Their Brave New World
Gummy Bear Detective
The Candy Detective
What Candies Fear
The Blurred Image
Shattered Legions
The First Rememberer
Life of A Rememberer
System of Wonder
Lifesaver
Remarkable Way She Died
The Interrogation of Annabella Stormic

Blade of The Emperor
Arbiter's Truth
Computation of Battle
Old One's Wrath
Puppets and Masters
Ship of Plague
Interrogation
Edge of Failure

Fantasy Short Stories:
City of Snow
City of Light
City of Vengeance
Dragons, Goats and Kingdom
Smog The Pathetic Dragon
Don't Go In The Shed
The Tomato Saver
The Remarkable Way She Died
Dragon Coins
Dragon Tea
Dragon Rider

WAY OF THE ODYSSEY STARTER COLLECTION

All books in 'An Introductory Series':
Clinical Psychology and Transgender Clients
Clinical Psychology
Careers In Psychology
Psychology of Suicide
Dementia Psychology
Clinical Psychology Reflections Volume 4
Forensic Psychology of Terrorism And Hostage-Taking
Forensic Psychology of False Allegations
Year In Psychology
CBT For Anxiety
CBT For Depression
Applied Psychology
BIOLOGICAL PSYCHOLOGY 3RD EDITION
COGNITIVE PSYCHOLOGY THIRD EDITION
SOCIAL PSYCHOLOGY- 3RD EDITION
ABNORMAL PSYCHOLOGY 3RD EDITION
PSYCHOLOGY OF RELATIONSHIPS- 3RD EDITION
DEVELOPMENTAL PSYCHOLOGY 3RD EDITION
HEALTH PSYCHOLOGY
RESEARCH IN PSYCHOLOGY
A GUIDE TO MENTAL HEALTH AND TREATMENT AROUND THE WORLD- A GLOBAL LOOK AT DEPRESSION
FORENSIC PSYCHOLOGY
THE FORENSIC PSYCHOLOGY OF THEFT, BURGLARY AND OTHER CRIMES AGAINST PROPERTY
CRIMINAL PROFILING: A FORENSIC PSYCHOLOGY GUIDE TO FBI PROFILING AND GEOGRAPHICAL AND STATISTICAL PROFILING.
CLINICAL PSYCHOLOGY

FORMULATION IN PSYCHOTHERAPY
PERSONALITY PSYCHOLOGY AND INDIVIDUAL DIFFERENCES
CLINICAL PSYCHOLOGY REFLECTIONS VOLUME 1
CLINICAL PSYCHOLOGY REFLECTIONS VOLUME 2
Clinical Psychology Reflections Volume 3
CULT PSYCHOLOGY
Police Psychology

A Psychology Student's Guide To University
How Does University Work?
A Student's Guide To University And Learning
University Mental Health and Mindset

Milton Keynes UK
Ingram Content Group UK Ltd.
UKHW050903210624
444436UK00015B/367